Husbands of the Outback

Two tough, powerful men
no woman can resist...

MARGARET WAY—Genni's Dilemma

Genni has loved cattleman Blaine Courtland since
childhood—so why is she about to marry another
man...and will Blaine really let her?

"With climactic scenes, dramatic imagery and
bold characters, Margaret Way makes the Outback
come alive."

—*Romantic Times*

BARBARA HANNAY—Charlotte's Choice

Lady Charlotte Bellamy is torn between love
and duty: to please her family, she must accept a
marriage of convenience, but her heart longs for
rugged rancher Matt Lockhart....

"Barbara Hannay's debut offers a pleasing premise
with engaging characters, wonderful tension and
good pacing."

—*Romantic Times*

D1007613

Margaret Way is a true legend in the world of romance writers and readers. She has been published for almost thirty years and is renowned for her strong, passionate characters and her wonderfully lyrical and evocative descriptions of Australia. She was born and educated in the river city of Brisbane, and now lives within sight and sound of beautiful Moreton Bay in the state of Queensland. She delights in bringing her country alive for readers. Prior to beginning her writing career, Margaret had a musical one—she was a pianist, teacher, singing coach and accompanist. She still plays the piano seriously; she also collects art and antiques and is devoted to her garden.

**Look out for
MASTER OF MARAMBA by Margaret Way (#3671)
On-sale October 2001**

Barbara Hannay was born in Sydney, educated in Brisbane and has spent most of her adult life living in tropical north Queensland, where she and her husband have raised four children. While she has enjoyed many happy times camping and canoeing in the bush, she also delights in an urban lifestyle—chamber music, contemporary dance, movies and dining out. An English teacher, she has always loved writing, and now, by having her stories published, she is living her most cherished fantasy.

**Look out next month for
OUTBACK WITH THE BOSS by Barbara Hannay (#3670)
On-sale September 2001**

MARGARET WAY
BARBARA HANNAY
Husbands of the Outback

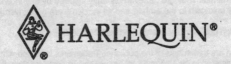

HARLEQUIN®

TORONTO • NEW YORK • LONDON
AMSTERDAM • PARIS • SYDNEY • HAMBURG
STOCKHOLM • ATHENS • TOKYO • MILAN • MADRID
PRAGUE • WARSAW • BUDAPEST • AUCKLAND

ISBN 0-373-03664-7

HUSBANDS OF THE OUTBACK

First North American Publication 2001.

Copyright © 2001 by Harlequin Books S.A.

GENNI'S DILEMMA
Copyright © 2001 by Margaret Way, Pty., Ltd.

CHARLOTTE'S CHOICE
Copyright © 2001 by Barbara Hannay.

This edition published by arrangement with Harlequin Books S.A.

® and TM are trademarks of the publisher. Trademarks indicated with ® are registered in the United States Patent and Trademark Office, the Canadian Trade Marks Office and in other countries.

Visit us at www.eHarlequin.com

Printed in U.S.A.

CONTENTS

Genni's Dilemma
by Margaret Way

Dear Reader,

It's with greatest pleasure I join Barbara Hannay in this special novel—*Husbands of the Outback*. It's a nice touch to team us together. Barbara is at the start of her career. I've been blessed with thirty wonderful years writing for Harlequin®. I've carved out a rewarding and thoroughly enjoyable career in the process, giving pleasure and comfort to many thousands of women all around the world. Could anyone ask for more?

Although I've written many books with different settings, my Outback stories are the ones my readership tell me they love best. Writing can be a solitary business, so it's lovely to get feedback from loyal fans. Through all my travels around my own great island continent, Australia, washed as it is by glorious blue oceans, it's the cloudless cobalt skies that speak directly to my heart. The great open, silent immensity of it! I stand in awe of the rugged grandeur, the starkly beautiful and dramatic landscapes. One has to see the beating Dead Heart then experience the wilderness after rain as the endless mirage-haunted plains are woven with wildflowers.

I want to share my feelings of utter bliss with you, my fascination with the great Inland, so absolutely, so distinctively Australian. The same with our Outback man. He's a unique breed. Full of strength and tremendous energy. The quintessential rugged male who still manages to exhibit an almost "old-worldly" gentleness and courtesy. Wonderful stories have been written about the pioneers of Outback Australia, inspirational and enthralling. I want to tell you the mighty Outback man hasn't disappeared. He's still out there for the rest of us to be proud of.

Margaret Way

CHAPTER ONE

The Wedding Eve

GENEVIEVE stood outside her mother's bedroom door bracing herself for the inevitable confrontation and, she guessed, copious tears. Angel was perfectly capable of it. Generally believed saccharine-sweet, no one knew better than Angel how to make a lot of people uncomfortable. She could turn it on. And off. At the flip of a coin.

Genevieve didn't know if she could stand it, feeling as bad as she did. After a month of agonizing about this soon-to-be-taken trip to the altar, she had lost weight to the point she was looking more spindly than slim; she had a permanent headache; she was sick to her stomach and trying to smile through it; her emotions so barely under control it hurt.

About to tap on the door and await entrée into her mother's opulent bedroom that stopped just short of mirrors on the ceiling, Genevieve suddenly remembered with a great sense of relief Angel was going out to dinner with Toby Slocombe. She marvelled she could have forgotten, but then her brain was firing on less than four cylinders.

Toby was one of the high rollers around Sydney Town, recently divorced from his long-suffering wife of thirty years. For once Angel hadn't been involved having just come out of a rather unsettling experience with a toy-boy a little older than her daughter. So tonight no tears to spoil the mascara. No tears to stain Angel's ravishing little heart-shaped face. Even so she wouldn't take it without a bit of light screaming and the usual attempt to talk Genevieve down. Genevieve felt she could just about endure that.

Angel's soft breathy voice raised a few decibels arguing nonstop. No one was home except Genevieve's beloved Emmy, their long-time housekeeper, baby-sitter, nanny, confidante, social secretary-assistant, referee, who had been more of a mother to Genevieve than Angel the perennial beauty and social butterfly had ever been.

This is supposed to be one of the happiest days of my life, Genevieve thought, avoiding all self-pity. Indeed she felt very isolated and quite guilty, tempted to do a runner. Please God help me through this, she prayed as she rapped on her mother's door, the great emerald-cut diamond on her left hand winking and blinking heavy enough to anchor a harbour ferry.

"Come!" her mother's voice trilled.

It was the sort of response one might expect from a celebrated prima donna, not a mother, Genevieve thought. Not a "Come in" much less "Yes, darling." Emmy, after all, was watching one of her favourite TV shows, not surprisingly, "The Nanny," and could not be disturbed. Not knowing whether to laugh or cry Genevieve opened the door, her eyes filled with the sight of her mother half falling out of a long sequinned evening dress in a heavenly shade of jacaranda that must have cost as much as the piece of antique furniture Genevieve was about to bump into.

"Lordy, Sweet Mamma," she said, amazed like everyone else by her mother's youthful appearance and all-out glamour.

Angel, the picture of seduction, threw out her slender arms and made a full turn. "Like it?"

"What there is of it, yes," Genevieve agreed slowly. "It's beautiful. Exquisite."

"I'd let you wear it only you're too tall," Angel instantly responded, smoothing the filmy fabric over her hips.

"I'm not *that* tall," Genevieve said. "Anyway, you've never lent me anything."

Angel sprayed herself with another whiff of gorgeous perfume. "Genni, sweetheart, you've never wanted for anything. I know you're beautiful, though I looked twice as good when I was your age, but you have your poor father's height. And that olive skin." Angel turned to survey her own flawless strawberries-and-cream complexion.

"Most people think my skin is great," Genevieve answered casually enough. She always took her mother's little put-downs with no offence. "Unlike you, I take a tan and it goes very well with my hair."

"Our hair," Angel corrected, touching her heavy white-gold naturally wavy locks. In her mid-forties, an age Angel kept quite secret even from her doctor, Angel wore her hair short, brushed up and away from her exceedingly youthful, marvellously pretty face. Genevieve wore hers long, sheets of it, falling to her shoulder blades. Sometimes she had it straightened but it inevitably went back into its waving skeins.

The two of them were very much alike despite the fact Angel was petite and Genevieve stood 5'8" in her stockinged feet with long, light limbs. Most people thought Genevieve was twice as beautiful as her mother and as a member of the Courtland family it was expected she would have brains, something her mother either didn't have or concealed. Not that it affected Angel's great ongoing success with men. In fact it might well have contributed to it.

"Genni, do you know what you're doing?" Angel broke sharply into her daughter's reverie.

"Nope, what am I doing?" Genevieve asked.

"You're handling that precious piece of Sevres so carelessly you might drop it. Please put it down."

"Sorry, Mamma."

"Darling, haven't I asked you not to call me that?"

Genevieve laughed, trying to cloak a lifetime's despair. "You're one tough lady, Angel. Do you know that? You asked me not to call you Mamma when I was barely ten years old. Not all that long after Daddy died." It was cruel.

Genevieve still thought it was cruel but she had never been one to start, in her own words, "a ruckus." Not being able to call her mother Mummy or Mum had not only been harrowing, it had somehow affected their relationship. Underneath it all Genevieve felt terrible sorrow her mother wasn't the complete woman.

In fact Angel was moaning now. "Oh, don't start that again." She always did at any mention of her late first husband, Genevieve's father, Stephen Courtland. Angel had divorced Stephan when Genevieve was seven. Eighteen months later he had been tragically killed in a shooting accident on Jubilee. Jubilee was the Courtland flagship, the desert fortress and ancestral home. The Courtlands controlled a cattle empire that cut a huge swathe through the giant state of Queensland. Blaine was the current custodian of the flame. Blaine Courtland, Genevieve's kissin' cousin, prince among men.

At thirty-one, handsome as the devil and just as arrogant, he was a much respected man in a tough man's world. Blaine had been the hero of Genevieve's childhood and early adolescence. Eight whole years separated them but they were light years away in substance and maturity.

The little girl Blaine had always called by a string of endearments: flower face, Violetta—because of her eyes—sweetness, cherub, little pal, even pumpkin—she remembered all of them—overnight turned into that silly little idiot Genni who was prepared to waste her perfectly good brain trying to emulate her fool of a mother. Blaine pulled no punches about Angel. He actually called her Jinx to her face. A lot of it stemmed from the fact the Courtland family collectively believed Stephen Courtland's "accident" had been no accident at all. Everyone knew Stephen had been devastated when Angel walked out on him, taking his adored only child. A serious depression had followed.

"Angel, can I talk to you?" Genevieve asked, picking up her courage.

"I don't really have time to talk now, darling," Angel said, hunting up her exquisite evening purse, popping in a fragile lace-edged hanky. "Shouldn't you be getting your beauty sleep? It's going to be a wonderful day tomorrow. I'm so proud of you landing Colin."

Genevieve received a mind picture of Blaine so searing it hurt her head. "I think I'll pass on Colin," she blurted abruptly.

"You'll what?" Angel's blue-violet eyes started so far from her head she looked like an adorable bug.

"I can't go through with it, Mamma... Angel. I feel terrible about it, I know it's what you want. What you've done everything in your considerable power to bring about, but I don't love Colin. I never did. I was going through with marrying him to spite Blaine. I can see that now."

Angel sat down heavily in a cream damask armchair, her tiny face blanching. "I'm not hearing this. I'm not!" she wailed. "What has this got to do with Blaine? You surely can't believe he'll be pleased about this. He's paid for the whole blasted thing."

She was betrayed. In that moment humiliation left her bereft. "He what?" Her desperation was almost total.

"Oh, don't play the fool. It doesn't work with me," Angel scolded with some contempt. "You surely didn't think I was going to outlay a small fortune. The Courtlands have a mountain of money. Blaine can well afford a lavish wedding for three hundred. A drop in the ocean to him. But it would leave a big dint in my bank balance."

"My God!" Genevieve could have howled with the pain. "You let me believe you were handling all this, Mother. Yes, *Mother*. You are my mother, aren't you? My father, God rest his soul, left you very well off. He loved you, the poor deluded man. He loved *me*. There has to be money, Mother. Look around this God-awful bedroom, this mansion of a house. Look at that dress you've got on. The diamonds in your ears and around your neck."

"Will you please stop making a commotion?" Angel wrung her hands. "I have to look after *myself*, Genevieve. I have many more years left to me."

"I thought you were working your head off to land Toby Slocombe?" Genevieve fired.

"Don't you dare scream at me, you ungrateful little wretch." Angel was furious and showed it. "How can you possibly let me down? Let Colin down? I don't dare think of the consequences."

"No." Genevieve shook her head violently, in agony. "Because you expected me to help out once I got my hands on the Garrett money. You know Colin's father is universally detested."

"I happen to know he approves of you," Angel said, tight-lipped with anger. "He's thrilled Colin has finally found someone who will be a good steadying influence on him."

"You've played us all like puppets," Genevieve said, recognizing it was true. "You might give some people the impression you're an airhead but you always get what you want, don't you, Mother?"

Angel had the grace to flush. "I don't know what's got into you, Genevieve. You haven't been the same since you got back from Jubilee. Of course it's Blaine. He's always so goddam polite, but I know he hates me. They all do. They blame me for Stephen. As though I was there when he tripped over that bloody fence. They're a revolting family. So uppity. The landed elite. Yet Blaine's own mother ran off. Dear Crystelle. Don't let him fool you. Blaine hates women."

Genevieve brushed a long ash-gold tendril from her face. "He was kindness itself to me."

"You mean when you were a little kid," Angel scoffed, jealous of Blaine's affection for her daughter to this day.

"A little *fatherless* kid. I loved Blaine with all my heart,"

Genevieve admitted, frightened somehow by the depth of her own emotion.

Angel gave a hard laugh. "Well, that's all gone by the board. You two have had a very difficult relationship for years now. The arrogance of the man! He has always interfered. You'd think he was your guardian, not me. Remember the time I wanted you to be a model. You could have been right up there at the top. An international career. You had everything going for you, but no, Blaine insisted you go on to university."

"I was a straight-A student, Angel," Genevieve reminded her. "I didn't want to be a model."

That struck Angel as irrelevant. "It's the best career a beautiful girl could possibly have. Such an exciting, glamorous life."

"So you say. It wasn't for me."

Angel's pretty mouth puckered. "So working at the State Art Gallery is better?"

"I have a Fine Arts Degree. I'm quite a good artist myself. I'm learning all the time. I'm regarded as a valuable addition to the team. All of this fades into the background now, Angel, I can't go through with this marriage."

That struck Angel as shocking. She burst into faintly hysterical laughter. "Not a chance you're getting out of it," she cried loudly. "Blaine will drag you down the aisle if he has to. Don't forget there's the honour of the Courtland name at stake."

Genevieve's violet eyes burned. "I'm only a cousin, Angel. Third cousin. I don't really count."

"Don't be so sure of that, my girl." Angel began to fiercely swing an evening-sandalled foot. "This would be the most appalling breach of social etiquette. It's unthinkable."

"Except if I go through with it I'll be making the most hideous mistake of my life," Genevieve said in a voice thin with despair. "Please listen to me, Angel. I feel so *alone.* Shaking inside."

But Angel was furious with her. "Who the devil *are* you, Genevieve?" she shouted. "Who are you really? You're certain of it? Why *now.* Why didn't you just leave it until tomorrow morning? Climb out the bathroom window. I know you've seen that movie with Julia Roberts. Jumping on horses. You've got cold feet. All brides have cold feet. A little surprise for you, darling. You simply cannot let any of us down. You're emotionally fragile, like your father."

At that Genevieve's violet eyes flashed into brilliant life. "Damn you, Mamma," she said. "Damn you for leaving my father in the first place. Isn't it enough that he's dead? You're going to defame him?"

"Now just hang on a minute," Angel hissed. "I'm not defaming anyone. I'm saying it the way it is. You started something. Finish it. You're going to go through with this marriage, Genevieve. Colin Garrett is a catch most girls would kill for. He's attractive, he's rich—or he will be, he always makes the best-dressed list, he's more 'in' than 'out' in all the glossies. He's ideal. I just love the way he kisses my fingertips every time he sees me. *Bellisima, Angelina!* he always says."

"Why don't you just tell him to shut up?" Genevieve continued angrily. "His mother won't be unhappy. I know in my heart she doesn't think we're suited. I think she thinks I might desert her darling boy sometime in the future. Like you deserted Daddy." Her voice quivered pathetically.

Angel tilted her head back, staring at the elaborately decorated plaster ceiling. "I didn't desert your father, Genevieve. I just moved out. I've never met a man so *needy* in my whole life. I found his love for me suffocating, his insistence on a 'home life'. The three of us doing things together. God, how dreary! Possessiveness can be pretty awful."

Angel stood up in a torment. "You've upset me,

Genevieve,'' she said. ''What a lousy thing to do. I accept you're uptight. It's certainly not unheard of. I strongly advise you have a glass of warm milk and go to bed. When you wake up in the morning you'll feel entirely different.'' She turned to face her daughter, who somehow looked fourteen years old. ''Now, Toby will be here shortly. I don't want to hear any more of this. I can't deal with it. I don't know either why you can't stand the idea of Blaine's paying for it all?''

''That's because you're a sponger, Mamma. You're good at it.'' Genevieve lifted her head, pinning her mother's gaze. ''But I'm going to hold it against you forever.''

''Are you?'' Angel exploded, sweet voice rasping. ''How dare you speak to me like this, Genevieve, you sanctimonious little twit. Blaine and I have been working together for years. He's a very complex character, is your hero. He hasn't approved of anything you've done these last couple of years yet he's more than happy to pick up all your bills.

''Oh, yes, darling, don't look so shocked. It might have been my deepest darkest secret, but Blaine has helped out a lot. Why not? He really did think you were a great little kid and he's notoriously difficult to please. And you're a Courtland. That's a huge thing in your favour. Blaine was happy to keep you in the appropriate manner.''

Genevieve felt like a hand was squeezing her heart. ''You asked him?''

Incredibly Angel became almost jovial. ''Not at all. He just did it. You were the entrancing little 'honey chile'. But I expect by now he'll be happy to let someone else shoulder the burden.''

A deep vivid rose stained Genevieve's golden skin. She looked up, her eyes as dark as the ocean, aware as she had never been before in her life deep inside her mother some odd malice moved. ''Don't say any more, Angel,'' she begged. She, too, stood up, straightening her shoulders.

"With any sort of luck after tomorrow we mightn't have to see one another again."

Angel heard the finality in her daughter's voice. "Dear, oh, dear, what a silly thing to say," she gushed. "I love you, Genni. I'm very proud of you." She swept forward to pat her daughter's face, wondering why when she was so pretty herself she always felt jealous of Genni's hair, her eyes, her mouth, the radiant smile never much in evidence these days, the lovely teeth. God she even wished she was taller, then she wouldn't have to diet so rigorously.

"The last thing in the world I want is for you to be unhappy, Genni," she said tremulously, ready to shed a few tears. "Trust me, darling, you're suffering from prenuptial nerves. It's normal, not a catastrophe. Colin is so nice. Such fun, and he'll be drowning in money. I've been responsible for you for so long you should feel some responsibility for me. I know tomorrow you're going to make us all very proud. It's my dream, honey."

After her mother had left in a flurry of breathless giggles, hanging on to Toby Slocombe's arm, Genevieve went in search of Emmy. Emmy was still sitting in front of the television in the small room off the library, watching an old movie, a half-eaten box of Belgium chocolates Genevieve had bought for her on her lap, short plump legs resting on an ottoman.

"Hello, darling girl." Emmy looked up to smile; her pleasure diminishing as she saw the anguish in Genevieve's expression. "Going to watch this with me?"

Despite herself Genevieve was amused. "God, Em, you must have seen this movie a hundred times?" She recognised Cary Grant and Eva Marie Saint. *North by Northwest.*

"Better than the ones they make these days," Emmy snorted. "Wasn't he just the handsomest man?"

"He surely was," Genevieve agreed. "Bisexual, I gather?"

"That's just talk." Em snatched up another chocolate. "He was a real man. Anyway, what's wrong with you? You look like you need a stiff drink when you should be looking blissfully happy."

Genevieve sat down, gripping her hands. "That's just it, Em. I'm not happy."

A pause, then Emmy said, "I was wonderin' when you were going to realise it." She used the remote control to switch off the television. "Want to talk about it?"

"I just tried talking to Angel," Genevieve muttered abruptly.

"I imagine that didn't go too well. It's a damn shame the way your mother has been pressuring you to marry Colin."

Genevieve shook her white-gold head, her hair caught back in a single thickly braided rope. "Don't blame Angel, Em. I did it myself." Genevieve lifted her beautiful eyes. "What do you really think of Colin, Em?"

Put on the spot Emmy finally owned up. "I'm with Blaine," she said, not wishing to add she thought Colin Garrett nowhere near good enough for her darling Genni. Such a good girl. A lovely girl. Never given an ounce of trouble. Emmy would have found another position years ago only for Genni.

"Forget Blaine," Genevieve whispered, tears starting to her eyes. "He's been *awful* to me."

"But we can't forget Blaine, poppet," Emmy said. "Come on, admit it. You love him, hate him, whatever. He's always been there for you. Yet I have the feeling both of you are still only tapping into what you really mean to each other."

Genevieve inhaled a deep lungful of air. "He's a tyrant. Bloody-minded. He has too much power. Angel just told me he's paying for the wedding, I suppose the wedding dress, the bridesmaids' dresses, the flowers, the photographers, the church, the marquees, the mountains of food, the drink, the lot.'' She turned her violet eyes on Emmy, who knew a great deal more than she ever said.

"And that's upset you?"

"Upset me?" Genevieve nearly gave way to a primitive urge to scream. "It's devastated me. I wonder what else my mother *is* capable of? I suppose he's paid for everything for years." She bit her lip hard, realizing she was on the verge of crying.

"Blaine really cares about you, Genni," Emmy pointed out very gently. "He may be a little short with you from time to time but he's always had your best interests at heart."

"Isn't that nice! He frightens me," Genevieve suddenly admitted in a wobbly voice.

"Why, sweetheart?" Emmy, maternal by nature but childless, leaned forward, concern on her sunny-natured face.

Genevieve held her aching head. "He's maddening. He's a maddening man. And he has a cruel streak."

"No. I can't let that go," Emmy answered with an emphatic shake of her head.

"You always take his part, Emmy. Even *you*."

"Because he's a fine man. I've been around you both a long time, Genni. I know how good Blaine has been to you."

Genevieve gave a miserable sigh, lost in the utter strangeness. She wanted Blaine so badly she was buckling under the strain. "So why has he turned against me, Em?"

"Why don't you ask him?" Emmy countered so vigorously she set her grey curls bouncing.

"What a joke." Genevieve hugged herself distractedly. "He's frozen me out, as you very well know."

Emmy nodded. "Something went very wrong that polo weekend."

Even remembering made Genevieve tremble the length of her. "It was just that... Oh, God, Em." She was drowning in the emotion that surfed through her blood. "Blaine was scathing when I told him I was going to marry Colin. He didn't take me seriously enough. Then he flew into a cold rage. Those glittering eyes! He told me we could never be happy. He must have thought my education needed broadening because he pulled me to him so absolutely ruthlessly. I thought he was about to beat me. Instead he kissed me, which was *worse!* I heard stars burst.''

Emmy swung her feet off the ottoman, looking at Genevieve clutching her cheeks. "Kissed you? So he's kissed you a million times.''

"Oh, yes, throwaway kisses? Pecks on the cheek. Weren't you listening, Em. I said *he kissed me.* Really kissed me. It rocked me to my soul. It was brutal. It was brilliant. It was horrible. I thought I was going to die.''

"My goodness!'' Emmy, knowing Blaine got the thrilling picture.

"There was *no* excuse for him,'' Genevieve said. "He did it in such a way he's ruined my life.''

"How's that, darlin'?'' Emmy asked with a great rush of protectiveness.

Genevieve looked back, startled. "Get real, Em. How can I possibly marry Colin when Blaine kissed me? I'm afraid of Blaine.''

"That powerful?'' Emmy looked at Genevieve with love and understanding. She adored the girl.

"He's turned my world upside down, Em. Maybe he didn't mean to. But he has. I was going along okay. But now! He's pierced me like an arrow. So strange when he's planning on getting married himself.''

Emmy closed the box of chocolates carefully. "I take it you mean Sally Fenwick?'' she asked briskly.

"Of course I mean Sally.'' Genni didn't look up. "She's lovely and kind. They've been very good friends for so long. Sally is coming to the wedding. She's staying at the same hotel. Even Hilary likes and approves of her.'' Genevieve referred to Blaine's prickly young stepsister, several years younger than herself. "Hilary hinted marriage isn't far off."

"Really? I thought it was a bit of a one-sided relationship," said Emmy levelly.

"That's because Blaine never gives anything away."

"He kissed you. Some kiss by the sound of it."

Genevieve's face flared. "Blaine does everything like that, though, doesn't he? He doesn't realise he's so..."

"Powerful?" Emmy hit on the right word.

"God I hate him!" Genevieve said in a small voice.

"Why don't you tell him?" practical Emmy suggested.

"I did." Genevieve barely whispered it. "I told him I wanted him out of my life. I told him I was sick to death of his dictatorial ways. I haven't been able to do a thing to please him for years."

"Why don't you tell him *again?* You might get through this time."

Genevieve considered this, then shook her head. "I won't see him until he walks me up the aisle."

"So tell him tonight," Emmy pressed. "What's wrong with that?"

"You mean go to his hotel?"

Emmy nodded. "If I were you I'd do it like a shot."

Genevieve stared at her. "Emmy, darling, what are you saying?"

"Maybe what I should have said before. Tell Blaine what you tried to tell your mother. You can't go through with this marriage."

Genevieve sat erect in her chair and looked at her dear friend in alarm. "He'd be shocked out of his mind."

"I wonder," Emmy countered briskly.

"No Courtland would do such a terrible thing. Call off a wedding at the last moment."

"It's healthier than making a dreadful mistake, poppet." Emmy leaned over to grasp Genevieve's arm. "Blaine's no ordinary man. Tell him what's in your heart. Let him take charge.''

Genevieve's lovely face looked stricken. "I don't know if I dare. This is dreadful, Em. The house is ready. The church is ready. Our dresses are hanging upstairs. Fabulous dresses that cost a fortune. Three hundred guests are coming. The presents are all in. I don't know if I have the courage. I don't think I can humiliate Colin and his family. Colin's father might very well line up a pantechnicon to run me over. He's the Freight King after all.''

"Listen, you've been bullied into this," Emmy snorted. "By Colin's steamroller of a father on the one hand and your conniving mother on the other. An engagement of a couple of months was diabolically clever. You haven't had time to know your own mind. But evidently Blaine's kissing you has changed it.''

Genevieve's face mirrored her inner havoc. "I felt something I've never felt in my life. I felt Blaine owned me body and soul. That he's always been waiting for me to grow up. One kiss ended our old relationship. Dear God, I thought we were *family*. But it wasn't family in my blood. I can't deny I always thought he was the most marvellous man in the world, so exciting he makes the air vibrate, but we were cousins. I was his little Violetta. Remember how he used to call me that?''

"Oh, golly, I remember everything." Emmy's voice was low and wry. "Blaine has quite a way with words. For a very commanding man, daunting man at times, Blaine has his softer side. He could be very tender with you. Go to him, poppet. Pour out your heart. I have a feeling he'd pull down the stars for you if you asked him. No, don't look at me like that. It's true.''

"It's not easy, Emmy," Genevieve said sadly. "I think Blaine wants our break to be permanent.''

Hilary Courtland caught sight of Genevieve the minute she entered the hotel. Just seeing her gave Hilary a queer feeling when she'd been having a good time. Genevieve was moving with the speed and grace of a gazelle but Hilary got the impression of a deep unhappiness. Trouble, Hilary decided. Genni was looking for someone. Who else could it be but Blaine?

"Say, isn't that your cousin?" Hilary's male companion asked with immense interest. They'd been tucked away in a banquette, enjoying a mild flirtation, when he heard Hilary's odd little gasp and caught her startled gaze. Intrigued, he turned his head to follow up on the direction.

"Yes, that's Genevieve," Hilary answered, her smile twisted, her tone a lot more revealing than she intended. Ever since she could remember Hilary had felt rancour towards Genevieve. She was Blaine's sister yet Genni was the one Blaine had always cared about. Genni of the huge violet eyes and Rapunzel hair. Tonight Genevieve was casually dressed, navy gold-buttoned blazer, pale blue shirt, blue jeans, sneakers on her feet yet she looked like the model for the latest Ralph Lauren collection; a glamour girl like her dreadful femme fatale mother.

"God, she's a beauty, isn't she?" her companion commented, quite tactlessly. "Drop-dead gorgeous! How could a guy like Colin Garrett, even allowing for the Garret money, win *her* heart?"

"Well he has!" Hilary answered tartly, rendered almost dumb by jealousy. She put the lemon squash she was nursing down heavily and jumped to her feet. Genevieve appeared to be moving toward the bank of lifts. She had to stop her before she reached Blaine. She had to break what was coming up.

"Don't go away." She tossed a false smile at her boyfriend. "I'll have a word with her and I'll be right back."

Her companion waved her off. "Take your time." In actual fact he felt cheated out of meeting the gorgeous Genevieve. What was she doing here alone this time of night? Whatever it was, it didn't suit Hilary. She looked upset. Perhaps trying to make sense of her cousin's unexpected appearance.

Hilary, a small pretty dark-haired, dark-eyed girl but without the Courtland stunning good looks and height, put on a burst of speed. She reached Genevieve just as she was about to step into a lift.

"Hey, Genni!" she called, using such an urgent tone people turned their heads.

"Hilary!" Genevieve turned about, doing her utmost to hide her dismay. For all her efforts to be friendly to Blaine's young stepsister she had long since realised Hilary would never like her. "What a surprise!"

"And where are you off to?" Hilary fixed Genevieve with big questioning eyes.

Genevieve felt most unwilling to confide in this moody girl but what excuse could she offer? "I wanted to see Blaine for a moment," she explained as casually as she could. "The receptionist said he was in."

"Actually he didn't go out." Hilary reached out confidentially for Genevieve's arm and drew her away. "He and Sally are making a night of it. They had dinner together in the hotel. He's with her now, if you know what I mean?" Hilary rolled her brown eyes expressively. "I'd leave whatever you wanted to ask him to the morning if I were you. You wouldn't want to embarrass them." She smiled her kitten smile.

God no! Genevieve felt pierced by an arrow, at that moment ready to flee.

"What is it, anyway? Maybe I can help you?" Hilary's voice had grown unabashedly affectionate as Genevieve's desperation slipped out.

"I don't think so, Hills."

"Try me." Hilary guided Genevieve to a couple of chairs. "You know you really will have to get over running to Blaine for help," she warned gently, unsuccessfully trying to keep her jealousy opaque. "This time tomorrow night you'll be a married woman." Hilary couldn't help herself. She smiled in broad triumph. "You'll be entering a new life. Your name will be Genevieve Garrett not Courtland. Isn't that thrilling?"

Quietly, Genevieve removed the other girl's small hand from her arm. She had never felt less thrilled in her life. "You've never liked me, have you, Hilary?" she said levelly, putting years of pretence to one side. "On this night of nights, please tell me. What have I ever done to you?"

Hilary burst into a cascade of tinkling laughter. "Oh, my, Genni, surely you know having you around changed my entire life. For the worse."

"In what way? Why on earth have you been afraid of me? I would never want to hurt you. We could have been friends. Good friends. We're cousins. We could have forged an unbreakable bond. But you would never let me get close."

"Why on earth would I when you had perfected the art of getting between me and my brother." Hilary's pretty face was set into unpleasant lines.

"You're talking nonsense, Hilary." Genevieve was feeling sicker by the moment. "It's so unfair. To me. To Blaine. He loves you."

"No, he doesn't. Not really. I don't touch his heart. What heart he has he has reserved for you. The fatherless child." Hilary gave in to the huge temptation to say her piece. "Hell, you seduced him when you were a kid. You even robbed me of my father's love." A little sob rose to her throat. "When Dad was alive you used to twist him around your little finger. He hardly noticed me. I was the changeling in the Courtland fold."

Genevieve felt she might burst out crying, too.

"Hilary how did you let all this bitterness grow in your heart? It's *not true*. Not any of it. How long have you felt like this?"

"Since forever."

"Poor Hilary! You're breaking my heart," Genevieve said and meant it.

"I don't think so."

"Absolutely," Genevieve replied, feeling like she was mortally wounded.

"That's why I'm glad your getting married." Hilary smiled almost genially. "I knew one day you'd be out of our lives."

"That's no way to talk." Genevieve rose to her feet in protest. "How can you feel like this, say such things to my face, and still come to my wedding?"

"Why?" Hilary looked up at Genevieve, brilliant malice in her eyes.

"Because dear, sweet, beautiful, Genevieve, it's the day my brother will give you away forever."

Hilary was still sitting there feeling slightly shaky, but thrilled to have dispensed with the fleeing Genevieve, when Blaine suddenly materialised beside her, almost making her jump out of her skin.

"Isn't that Genni?" he demanded in the kind of voice that demanded a straight answer.

It took a tremendous effort for Hilary to pull herself together. How could she deny it? That white-gold rope of hair, the model figure, the grace of movement. "Yes, she just popped in to say hello." She tried a blithe smile, thinking fast.

"Damned odd." Blaine looked like he was about to take after her, such a restless radiance about him.

"Not really." Hilary rose, grasping her stepbrother's arm. "She and her bridesmaids were having a girl's night out. That was Genni's BMW parked out the front. Not supposed to do it, of course, but trust Genni to pull it off. A pity. You just missed her."

"And how was she?" Blaine bent his light lancing glance on his stepsister.

"Oh, lovely! Deliriously happy." Hilary turned an innocent face to him. "I've never seen a girl so much in love."

"The little fool!" Blaine's hard, handsome mouth tightened. "He'll never make her happy."

"But he *will,* Blaine," Hilary insisted, hugging her brother's arm. "She's the love of his life!"

And we're finally free of her.

"Don't," Blaine warned, his voice so strange Hilary stared at him vaguely terrified.

"Where's Sally?" she asked in an effort to divert him.

"She went home an hour ago." Blaine was still frowning, looking more formidable by the minute. "Surely you knew? We went right past you and your friend."

"I must have missed you," Hilary lied. "Sally's a darling. Mum and I are delighted she's the woman in your life."

"Don't be so dim-witted," Blaine responded impatiently, his eyes silver chips in his arresting dark face. "Your mother thinks no such thing. As for you? A bit of wishful thinking. Are you sure that's all Genni wanted?" he insisted. "To say hello?"

"What else?" Hilary wanted to turn and bolt, instead she lightly punched his shoulder. "She's on top of the world. I *am* family."

"So why did you turn down the role of bridesmaid?" Blaine challenged, giving her that lancing look that always made her feel so exposed.

She tried to make a joke of it. "You know. Genni's so tall. So are her friends. I didn't want to be the little pipsqueak in the middle. Genni understood. Come and join us for a minute." Hilary had a powerful nervous urge to draw her stepbrother away.

"No thanks." Blaine glanced down at her. "I want to

leave a message at the desk. Goodnight, Hills. Sweet dreams.''

She stood on tiptoe to kiss his lean cheek. "You, too, brother mine. It's going to be a wonderful day tomorrow. Like Genni, *I can't wait.*''

CHAPTER TWO

The Wedding Day

GENEVIEVE'S four bridesmaids, Tiffany, Montana, Penelope and Astrid, were scattered across her mother's enormous bedroom chattering and laughing, high on excitement, making minute adjustments to their bridesmaid gowns in a glorious palette of turquoise, fuchsia, lilac and violet, fanning out the voluminous silk skirts, tweaking the short sleeves that ballooned out from the ravishing off-the-shoulder necklines, smoothing the narrow tapered waistlines—all of the girls had been on a strict diet for a month: light breakfast on the day, absolutely nothing until the reception—settling their beautiful floral headpieces, works of art in themselves that matched the colour spectrum of their gowns. Each wore a necklace of twisted palest pink freshwater pearls with the clasp worn to the front, specially chosen to compliment their wonderful dresses—blue topaz, pink tourmaline, amethyst, sapphire—all set in an 18-carat-gold bezel, gifts from the bridegroom, Colin Garrett, heir to George Garrett, the Freight King.

"You should think about getting into your dress now, Genni," Angel urged, feeling a mite cross at her daughter's inappropriate lack of enthusiasm. "It's getting seriously late." She turned to waggle her fingers at the chief bridesmaid, Tiffany, a statuesque honey-blonde, who walked into Angel's dressing room "the size of a department store with twice as much merchandise" as Tiffany had confided to her mother and emerged holding Genni's gown aloft.

"Here comes the bride," Tiffany tried to speak playfully

30

but she, too, was perturbed by the look in her friend's eyes, so poignant it was painful to behold. It couldn't just be nerves. Genevieve looked very much like she didn't want to get married. Not to Colin Garrett anyway despite the fact many women including Tiffany herself found Colin very attractive.

"Wow!" Montana gave a mesmerized gasp as the others crowded around. "It's so beautiful it takes my breath away."

"Me, too!" Astrid agreed, visibly affected. Five times a bridesmaid, she was starting to feel like she was being passed over. But what a gorgeous creation was this gown! Thousands of seed pearls, tiny rhinestones and crystals glimmered on the tight-fitting off-the-shoulder ivory silk bodice, an exquisite pattern that was repeated around the hem of the beautiful billowing skirt.

"I can't wait to see you in it, Genni." Astrid, her shiny dark hair gathered into a deep upturned roll at the nape, looked towards her friend. "It's so absolutely you. I have to see you in it. Come on. You're so nervy you're turning me white."

Genevieve managed to laugh as she always laughed at her friend Astrid. "It seems to me I'm giving my life away."

Obediently she lifted her long slender legs exquisitely shod in handmade satin courts, stepping into her gown and standing perfectly still while her mother made short work of the long zipper in the back.

"Good God, Genni you've got terribly thin," Angel protested, giving an exasperated sigh. "The waistline could do with another tuck."

"It's all right," Genni insisted, edging away quietly. "Don't fuss, Angel. I want no fuss."

"All right, my darling. All right." Angel trilled, adopting a rare motherly tone to counteract Tiffany's look of veiled censure. Cheek of the girl! Someone should remind her of her manners. Angel continued to stare into her daughter's face, feeling a cold wave of panic.

Genevieve had tried to open her heart to her but she hadn't wanted to listen. *Still* didn't for that matter. She was so bloody desperate to get Genevieve married off to the right man. Someone who knew how to respect a beautiful mother-in-law and shower her with gifts. But under the silky golden tan she always had in summer Genni was very pale, her violet eyes so huge they dominated her small face. They seemed to be the only colour about her. Maybe her lipstick, in a luminous frosted rose, needed a heavier application, a touch more blusher? Angel concentrated hard.

"Now the veil!" Montana, the only one not feeling the tension or misinterpreting it as normal bridal jitters approached carrying the full-length tulle veil tenderly over her arm. The headpiece of three exquisite full-blown silk roses, pink and cream with touches of gold was already set in place. Genni was wearing her hair long and loose, the natural curl exaggerated by her hairdresser to suit the romantic conception.

"All right, sweetie?" Montana, very pretty with short caramel-coloured hair, looked at her friend carefully. A number of expressions flitted across Genevieve's face. Enough to suddenly make warning bells go off in Montana's head. Colin was very rich, a lot of fun, but admittedly he couldn't hold a candle to someone like…someone like…well, someone like Genevieve's cousin, for instance, Blaine Courtland, the big cattle baron. But he was *family*, the man who was giving Genevieve away. The man due to arrive in about ten minutes at the house.

"Genni's a bit stressed." Angel threw her daughter a bracing look. "Big weddings are always like this." Together she and Montana adjusted the full-length two-tiered tulle veil edged with the finest band of crystals.

"You look truly beautiful, Genni. You bring tears to my eyes." Montana very gently kissed her friend's cheek. "I wish you all the happiness in the world. One thing's certain, Colin will always make you laugh. If he hadn't fallen in love with you I'd have been after him myself.''

"You were after him, darling,'' Astrid slipped in somewhat tartly.

Montana snorted in self-derision. "With Genni around I didn't stand a chance.''

"Hold up your head, Genni!'' clucked Angel, looking absolutely delicious not to say saucy in a light-as-air, sheer-as-silk aquamarine chiffon with swirls of gold and a colour-matched confection on her head that looked like some fabulous intergalactic butterfly had landed. "And do please try to smile.''

Genevieve wasn't sure she could. Conflicting emotions were threatening to overthrow her and she was starting to feel stomach cramps. On one level she couldn't bear to be the cause of a dreadful scandal, the gossip columns would outdo each other in their efforts to blame her. Mention would be made of her notoriously fickle mother. She couldn't bear to bring pain and humiliation to the perennially light-hearted Colin. He trusted her. He wanted her. She wasn't absolutely sure he loved her. He certainly hadn't shown her an excess of passion. She knew that now.

He didn't like the way she was embroiled in the art scene, either. He gave no sign he was interested in her artistic talent, or indeed any artistic talent at all. She'd once dropped the name Jason Pollock into the conversation and Colin thought he was a property developer. His father, George Garrett, was certain to go ballistic. Even now she could hear his great booming voice in her ears, but George Garrett was the least of her worries.

She felt such a fool. Yes, fool was the right word. And one she had to live with. A fool nursing pure loss.

Blaine, as always, was right. She only wished to God he had never kissed her. Before that it had been so easy to hide from herself. Now she felt thoroughly exposed for what she was, a woman prepared to go through with a marriage because the groom had been extremely nice to her. Of course that could be attributed to the emotional deprivation of her childhood. How could she ever have imagined she was *in love* with Colin?

She was beginning to wonder if she even knew what love was. Overnight she'd turned into a different woman. She knew the why and when. That was when she should have found the courage to act instead of waiting until three hundred guests had put on their wedding finery and left for the church. She either had to go through with it to avoid a terrible mess or lock herself in her bedroom and refuse to come out. If only she could have spoken to Blaine last night. She had so desperately wanted to.

Weeping inwardly, she realised she had to summon up the strength to wipe Blaine from her mind. Blaine had his own life. His marriage to Sally was coming closer, as Hilary had confided. Genevieve just knew she couldn't bear to be around when that happened. Blaine was lost to her. The very thought got her moving. An action that had Angel muttering a short prayer of gratitude.

"Party time!" she cried. "I'm not sure if you're not the most beautiful bride I've ever seen in my life."

"Some people have all the luck," Astrid murmured in an aside to Tiffany, which wasn't exactly the most appropriate response.

"Well, let's get moving people." Angel clapped a little sharply. Exquisitely fashioned at a scant five-feet-nothing, Angel was nevertheless temperamental, demanding, something of a bully as Emmy could and did attest. "You look gorgeous, all of you," she cooed, revelling in her soon to be new status of adored mother-in-law. "One final inspection before you go out the door. I can't believe the big day has finally arrived."

Floating down the giant central marble staircase that would have done justice to Scarlett O'Hara, Tiffany wished she'd surrendered to an early desire to talk her friend out of this marriage. "Angel's euphoria doesn't appear to have worn off on Genn. She looks like she wants to do a runner," she whispered to Astrid, who by way of response grabbed Tiffany by her beautiful ballooning sleeve.

"Perfect! If Genn doesn't want to marry him he can marry me."

And there was worse to come. Downstairs Blaine Courtland had arrived. He stood in the marble-floored, flower-bedecked entrance hall, peonies, lilac branches, delphinium, roses, perfect carnations, looking upwards with eyes as brilliant as diamonds. He wore the traditional grey frock coat, grey trousers, waistcoat and a sapphire-blue satin cravat with a diamond stickpin, but his stunningly handsome face sported no smile. Indeed it appeared he, too, didn't feel like a wedding, although it was common knowledge on the grapevine he had paid for the whole thing.

"God, isn't he brilliant! The cattle baron," Montana muttered to Penelope. She was thrilled to be moving in such a world of wealth and glamour. "I'm mad about dark smouldering types with a cleft in their chins. Purple passion, you know." She gave Penelope a rather awful dig in the ribs.

"He's spoken for, darling," Penelope reminded her. "Sally Fenwick. Well-known pastoral family. Minor royalty."

"Wouldn't we all like to be," Montana groaned. "But shouldn't someone remind him it's a wedding we're going to. He looks a bit scary. *For-mi-dab-leh* as the French would say. I tell you, Tiff, there's something going on."

It was certainly starting to look like it. Genni didn't look happy. Neither did her cousin who exactly fitted the picture of the sort of man Genni should have married, Tiffany thought even as she recognised that simply wasn't on.

For as long as Tiffany had known Genni, coming up twelve years now, Genni had idolized her cousin, although of recent years Genni had confided he had hurt her badly by treating her as though she wasn't really capable of managing her own affairs. "He can be awfully rough on me!" Tiffany remembered Genni's exact words. This marriage had to be one of those times. Both young women in their conversations had made extravagant attempts to steer clear of any rapids. It was Angel who had engineered the whole wedding, Tiffany suddenly realised, making glorious lovers out of just good friends.

Her heart labouring in her chest, Genevieve hugged the polished railing as she made her way slowly down the staircase to the magnificent gallery-style entrance hall supported by massive marble columns. Angel was seriously into drama though to Genni's eyes there was always an over-abundance of everything.

But on this day of all days she didn't notice the artworks, the soaring fresco ceiling, breathtaking chandelier and grand golden console and mirror with so much ormulu it would have looked a whole lot better at Versailles. She only had eyes for Blaine. Loving him as she now found she did had to be her tragic secret. He looked magnificent but so stern-faced staring up at her, such a glitter to his eyes she felt like she was drowning in a silver lake.

Yet when she finally reached him, as though drawn by a powerful magnet, he bent his crown black head to kiss her cheek. "Hello, cherub," he murmured. "You look exquisite. I knew you would." His voice dropped lower, for her ears only. "I want to tell you, Genni, I'll always be here for you. No matter what happens. I'll never let anyone hurt you. Or make you unhappy."

She made a small sound of agony, her violet eyes burning in her pale face. "Oh, Blaine! Why couldn't I talk to you last night?" she implored.

Instantly his black brows drew together and his lean powerful body radiated a kind of menace. "You wanted to talk to me when you came to the hotel?" he questioned, his voice with an imperative note to it.

Electric tension seemed to be flashing all around them. It was in his face, in his remarkable eyes. She was afraid where it could lead. "It's all right, Blaine." Her voice vibrated a little wildly. "All right. It would have been too late anyway."

"What?" He grasped her two hands and took them firmly in his own. "I need to know what you mean, Genni? Don't be afraid."

But I am afraid, she thought passionately. Afraid of you and what you mean to me. Afraid of my own feelings that have grown and grown like some monstrous secret flower.

"All right there, Blaine, Genni?" Angel who had been concentrating on fastening the clasp of her diamond bracelet that matched the sunburst on her shoulder now called, shooting anxious eyes at them. She had always been aware on some deep unprobed level Blaine and her daughter shared an unbreakable bond.

Blaine ignored her, his entire attention focused on Genni. "Genni, you've got to tell me the truth." His voice was low and taut. "Do you love this man?"

There was a moment of rushing silence. It was now or never. Then she remembered Sally. Sally at this year's celebratory Polo Ball with Blaine's gorgeous orchid pinned to her evening dress. Sally beaming with pride as people turned to see her and Blaine together. Sally looking for Blaine the moment he moved out of sight, eyes moving rapidly around the room. Sally hugging his arm.

"I must do, Blaine," Genni answered quietly. "I'm going to marry him."

"This is something you really want?" Clearly he still didn't believe her.

"God, Blaine, you're so unrelenting." Wanting to punish him as he had punished her, she spoke fiercely, in so much pain, so much pride, it was important she stop him from questioning her further. It was all too late. Colin had pursued and won her. Not Blaine. No matter what, Blaine was lost to her.

"I'm sorry." He dropped her hands at once, his dark high-mettled face now closed against her. "Forgive me. I wish you all the happiness in the world."

"I know you don't," Genni found herself responding wildly, too far gone to care. They were almost on the verge of one of their monumental arguments.

"Be careful what you say," Blaine warned, his eyes narrowed to mere slits.

In the entrance hall everyone stood around absolutely enthralled by what was going on between Genni and her commanding cousin. Although no one could make out what was being said, the body language told them heaps. There was grief, anger, and hurt, a raging that looked like antagonism. Genni's face was still very white but a high colour burned her cheeks. From stillness she had burst into abandoned brilliant life.

It wasn't looking good. Angel had the dismal feeling the two of them might just up and away. On the point of desperation, concerned for their every move, Angel stepped in. "Photographs people!" She turned swiftly to snap her fingers at the society photographer, Bernard, famous for his designer weddings, who gave no indication whatsoever he saw or heard her. "Then we really should be leaving for the church."

"There's time, Angelica." Blaine glanced briefly at his watch feeling like a lion wanting to protect its young. No one was going to *push* Genni into marriage. "Anyway, isn't it fashionable to be late?"

It was unless one had a great deal of worry on one's mind. Blaine was a man capable of anything, Angel thought, hustling them all into the spectacular formal living room with its breathtaking views of Sydney Harbour.

"You're over here, Blaine, next to me," she cooed, hoping to God Blaine would calm down.

Such was the severity of Blaine Courtland's expression everyone was amazed when he actually crossed the floor to tower over the petite Angel, five-three, and she was wearing high heels.

"I don't like the way Genni is acting," he told Angel, staring across the room at her. "If she's not entirely happy about this marriage, there's still time to bail out."

Just when Angel had a horror Genni was about to do just that. "Blaine, darling, you can't be *serious?*" A superb actress, she sounded amazed. "Every single day Genni has been telling me how happy she is. How much she loves Colin. They were made for each other. Soul mates!"

"Rubbish!" Blaine corrected very bluntly. "When you're madly in love with someone you don't look like Genni does now. I know her too well."

"But goodness, darling, you've never *been* madly in love with anyone, so how would you know?"

"Simple. You really should take time off to try and understand your daughter. Anyway, any woman I've been involved with is still my friend, which is a damned sight more than you can say of your two husbands and assortment of gigolos."

"You loved saying that, didn't you, darling?" Angel, unfazed by the hard truth, pulled a little face. "Sometimes, Blaine, you can be absolutely dreadful."

"When Genni's happiness and well-being is put on the line, yes," he acknowledged brusquely. "Look at her, Angel. Forget yourself and your plans. Look at Genni. She's as white as a snowdrop." His glittering grey gaze was directed to the centre of the overly grand room where Genni was being posed by Bernard in front of the white marble fireplace. It was adorned with a great abundance of white roses and green tracery topped and outdone by a large portrait of Angel in a deliciously low-cut blue-satin ballgown painted during the halcyon days of her ill-fated first marriage.

"God, I don't believe this," Blaine muttered blaming himself for not simply kidnapping the bride. A hundred vivid memories of Genevieve flitted through his head. The adorable two-year-old with her radiant violet eyes and riot of platinum curls.

He'd been ten years old when his father's favourite cousin, Stephen, had brought his little daughter to Jubilee. A difficult ten-year-old, hard to handle. A boy who already knew despair because his beautiful mother had abandoned him and his father and run off with her lover. An event so unexpected, so out of character, he sometimes thought he was still in a state of shock.

Genni had come into his life at the right time. Over the years he had given her all the love his heart could hold. She was so innocent, so vulnerable, so sweet-sassy intelligent, so generous with her affections.

As Stephen and Angel drifted further and further apart Genni had come to spend more time at Jubilee where she was back with her "cherished" Blaine. How close they had been then. It seemed he had taught her everything. How to swim, how to ride, how to handle a gun, how to find her way around the bush, how to survive. What he hadn't been able to teach her was how to pick the right men. In fact from about seventeen he'd been in despair about Genni's choices. Not a one good enough for her.

Certainly not Garrett, though loaded with money and a certain easy charm, he was short on substance. The more he had tried to tighten his hold on her, the more Genni had flown into little wild rages, claiming where he had once loved her now she was always in high disfavour. It wasn't true. He was hungry in spirit for the old easy relationship, but over the past few years an odd constraint had grown between them neither of them seemed to know how to break. Genni no longer ran to him for advice and comfort. Or did she? What was she doing at the hotel last night? Hilary had told him Genni had paid the visit to her. He should have known better about his stepsister's wiles. The unfortunate truth was Hilary had a deep-seated jealousy of Genevieve. Everyone in the family knew it, just as they knew Hilary had grown into her own worst enemy.

While Blaine brooded, his eyes like jewels, Angel was saying quite merrily, "Genni looks perfectly happy to me, darling. A touch of bridal jitters, no more." She reached up to pat Blaine's lean tanned cheek. "You're worrying about nothing," she said softly. "You always did have a powerful urge to keep Genni to yourself." Angel smiled as she watched Bernard straighten Genni's long beautiful veil. "Isn't her bouquet fabulous?" She smiled proudly. "You can't beat Hughie Rickman for flowers."

Blaine answered with such terseness it could easily have been interpreted as profound disapproval. "She's the most beautiful thing I've ever seen, but no one, not even Genni herself, can convince me she's in love with this guy. I can't have her marrying a man she doesn't love."

At the sweep-all-before it note in his voice, Angel put a trembling hand to her breast. Only for her deep concern for her makeup she would have been in tears. "Blaine, maybe you've got a problem," she suggested. "Genni hasn't." She lifted her face to him, despite herself pierced through with his wondrous blue-blooded aura. "You can't always run her life. You're here to give her away, my dear. In under a half hour you and Genni are going to do the grand march down to the altar. I know both your lives will change, but look on the bright side. You won't have to worry about her any more. You won't have to pick up all the bills." She said it totally without embarrassment, but Blaine answered with the merest lick of contempt.

"We're not talking about money. Everything would be fine if only I could believe Genni is marrying the man she loves."

His radar was working too well. "Blaine, darling," Angel tried her most convincing voice, tilting back her head so she could look him directly in the eye. "My daughter told me only last night never in her life has she been so happy." Telling fibs was one of Angel's lifelong specialities. "And she'll never want for anything, isn't that wonderful?"

Apparently that didn't thrill Blaine at all. "Who the hell cares about that?" he retorted in a low burned-up voice. "She couldn't be stupid enough to marry just for money?"

Angel was amazed by such a view. "That's all very well for people who have tons of it," she responded. "Money is way too good to pass up."

Blaine gave a weary sigh. "I just hope your outlook hasn't rubbed off on Genni," Blaine responded tautly. "There's much too much to her for the likes of Garrett. I liked him well enough when Genni first brought him to Jubilee but I never thought for one minute he was the man she was seriously considering marrying."

It was hard indeed to sound nonchalant. "Go on, darling," Angel teased. "I'm sure Genni tried to tell you. I know you really care about her but you don't show her much tenderness. The truth is your father's daunting manner spilled over on you. Genni fell head over heels in love with Colin. The only person who *didn't* know about it was you." Angel gave her tinkling laugh that held quite an edge.

It was Bernard the society photographer who halted Blaine's searing retort. "Pardon me?" Bernard called, struggling with his own radar. "It's your turn now, mother of the bride." He bowed gracefully in Angel's direction, though he hadn't taken to her one bit, "and the bride's very distinguished cousin, the well-known cattle baron, Mr. Blaine Courtland. I can't let *you* get away."

"God!" Blaine muttered beneath his breath, feeling Angel's small hand sneak into his as though he was too, too dear to her. In a few minutes he would have Genni alone in the car. He would be as gentle as he knew how with her. Angel's reference to his "lack of tenderness" had really stung. It was deserved. He was desperate now to get Genni to reveal her heart. He knew precisely how *he* felt. Every atom of his being was steeled against giving her away. If his instincts were correct beneath that exquisite bridal exterior Genni was screaming for help.

Inside the stretch limousine Genni sat very quietly in all her wedding finery, the billowing silk skirt stretched out over the seat, her veil arranged to one side lying in a foaming cloud atop it, looking determinedly out the window. If she dared to chance a look at Blaine sitting opposite her, he would recognise her despair. Even now she was fighting hard to keep the tears from welling into her eyes.

"Blaine," she said soundlessly over and over, trying to draw strength from just his name "I love you. I'll always love you." The knowledge was like a physical blow to the heart. Without food—she hadn't been able to eat a bite of breakfast—she felt dizzy and disoriented, caught up in a scenario Angel might well have written. I can't do this to myself. I can't do this to Colin, Genni agonised. He mightn't adore the ground I walk on but he deserves better than a wife who doesn't love him.

She started violently when Blaine suddenly reached over and caught her hand. "God, Genni. You'd think you were a winter bride. Your hands are freezing." He began to rub them, warming them in no time because her blood caught fire. "Angel took me to task back at the house. She told me a truth about myself I had to hear. I haven't been terribly kind to you of late, have I? As your mother put it, I haven't shown you much tenderness."

The admission nearly annihilated her. There was such a sparkle of tears behind her eyelids. "I haven't been very nice, either," she whispered. "The strange thing is, I don't have a temper with anyone else but you. You make me fly apart."

"That much, cherub, is obvious," he said dryly. "I know I'm too high-handed, too dismissive of what seems to me frivolous stuff. You have to make allowances for me. The thing is, Genni, I'm committed to something really important. *Your happiness.* No, don't shrink away from me,'' he begged as she leaned back and shut her eyes so aware of him she felt he was invading her. Body and soul. ''I know you, Genni. I used to know you, anyway,'' he added wryly, with that irresistible sparkle in his beautiful eyes she so loved. ''Just tell me once more—the last time, I promise— tell me you love Colin. That your dearest wish is to marry him?''

Such was her emotional state Genni had difficulty remembering Colin's face. ''Please, Blaine, can you stop asking me?''

''No.'' He shook his dark head. ''If you're frightened you must go through with this, just tell me. I'll take care of everything,'' he told her with that hard masculine authority. ''It'll be a nine-day wonder but there will be life after.''

Will there? Genni's thoughts went back to Sally Fenwick. ''Hilary told me you and Sally are coming around to setting your own wedding date?'' Once more she averted her head, looking sightlessly out the window.

Blaine turned her head back to him, loving and hating the sight of her in her glorious wedding dress. ''Is that what Hilary said to you last night?'' he demanded, his tanned skin lit by anger.

''She might have.'' Genni, too, was flushed; upset enough to jump out of the car. ''Please, Blaine, don't torment me. It would mean everything to me if you could respect how I feel.''

''When your heart is racing? When I can gauge what you feel through my palm?'' His laugh was low and savage. ''If it weren't so goddam lunatic I'd believe you're trying to get back at me for kissing you. There's no one, but *no one* like you for doing that.''

''Then why *did* you?'' Her breath trembled in her throat. ''It shocked me so much I nearly fainted.''

"I remember," he reminded her bitterly. "I was there."

"*Why*, Blaine?" She stared at him with her violet eyes, the urge to know consuming her. "You changed everything in a few moments." The power and the cruelty of the man!

"Did I?" He put his hands to either side of her, making her a prisoner. "You think about that, Genni. With my mouth on yours it didn't feel like you didn't want it."

Overwhelmed, she looked down. "And you betrayed Sally!"

He made a sound of complete exasperation. "Don't be so damned silly. Sally is a friend. A good friend, but she's not a woman I'd dream about. I've never cared about anyone like I care about you."

"Yes, as your little pet. Not a grown-up *woman*."

"We're not back to that again, are we?"

He drew away from her, his luminous eyes pure silver.

"Not *ever*. You've got some idea I can't live without you. But I've got news for you." Her words shrilled and trembled so, she was grateful for the glass panel that separated them from the chauffeur. *"I'm going to marry Colin."* Even as she said it she despised herself.

"And make a mess of your life?"

"You're so nasty, so…caustic…"

"Sad to say I am, just as you're so provocative. You know the dark depths in me, Genevieve. You're as used to my outbursts as I am to yours. I don't know about the chauffeur, if he can hear us. I haven't handled you particularly well of recent times. For that I genuinely apologise. It has all come out so badly because I couldn't seem to reach you. You were dead set on defying me at every turn. In fact you gave me hell."

There was truth at the heart of it. She could see it clearly now. "Don't. I love you," she admitted passionately. "I'm sorry. I'm sorry. Am I making any sense at all?"

"I'm afraid not." His answer was crisp. "You're not happy. That's obvious. You need a man who can set you alight. Do you think I haven't seen you incandescent? Women are such strange creatures. I'll never understand them." He said it like it might have been a curse.

Forlornly, Genevieve touched the exquisitely decorated bodice of her wedding gown. "Why did you never tell me you were paying for all this?"

He closed his eyes against the surge of hot anger. "I wish to God your mother could keep her mouth shut."

"I feel seared by shame."

"How ridiculous!" He sounded thoroughly stirred up. "You're family." God, that's *wrong*. For a moment he couldn't speak. Then as he glanced out the window he was shocked to see they had arrived at the church. Media photographers were in attendance, standing slightly apart from the crowd of onlookers that had gathered to see a bride well known to them through the social pages.

The bronze-polished skin on Blaine's face was stretched taut. "I'm not the kindest person in the world, Genni, but I'm here for you." His expression suggested only one word. *Action.* "Unless you're going happily into this, it would be better, far better, to stop it now."

For a moment hope glimmered, then she heard the oohs and aahs of the crowd. "For God's sake, Blaine, I'd be a social outcast. Help me to go through with it."

"Are you crazy?" He could crush her to him with one arm. Drag her away.

"Yes." She was finished and she knew it. Her mind reeled as the chauffeur came round to open her door. She could see her old life slide by. People were moving closer, waving and smiling, the photographers already shooting their pictures.

Please God help me, she prayed devoutly. Help me out before it's too late. I know I deserve this but I truly didn't understand my own heart.

That same heart bursting, Genevieve found herself standing out on the footpath to much applause while the designer of her gown fussed around her, settling her billowing silk skirt, adjusting her long froth of a veil.

"Isn't she beautiful!" came time and again from the crowd, but Genni didn't register the compliments. She felt she had the weight of the world on her shoulders instead of her wedding veil.

"Well?" Blaine gave her his arm, hovering over her inches over six feet, devastatingly handsome, the man who was to give her away, but the expression in his shimmering eyes was anything but family.

I'll love you always. Had she spoken it or thought it?

Only she had not known, had not understood that love at all.

What was going on here? Warren Maitland, the dress designer, thought in amazement. He simply couldn't *imagine* but his gown, his creation was gorgeous. So was the bride who looked like she mistook the cousin, the man who was to give her away, for the bridegroom. Maitland didn't believe any girl could look at a man like that and not be madly in love with him. In that moment, a trained observer, he sensed major scandal looming.

As if under a spell Genni found herself walking into the wonderfully picturesque old church, leaning into Blaine and on his arm. Where their flesh touched, it *burned.* It all had the quality of a dream to her. She could hear the music, the emotive swell of the organ; she could see her bridesmaids just inside the church. The elegantly dressed guests seated in the pews, so *many* of them, some had jetted in from overseas. Oh, God, for what? The pews were decorated with white satin ribbons. The altar luminous with white roses. Colin was waiting up there. Colin and his friends. She breathed and breathed, but she couldn't get enough air. She was going away...fainting...in front of her eyes a field of stars. The last thing she heard was Blaine saying her name...

If Genni hadn't solved the dilemma herself Blaine would have simply scooped her up, locked her to him, to face the

Furies. The wretchedness in her had been transmitted by the curled-up fingers on his arm. He felt her response in every nerve. It had pierced him through the heart.

What was done was done, he thought. He moved with incredible swiftness to gather the swooning bride up into his arms, her beautiful veil floating like a cloud above the waves of breezes that blew in the Gothic doorway. With high relief he saw his cousin Marc, a medical man, rush down the aisle to Genni's aid, the bridesmaids parting like fields of flowers at his approach. They weren't going to wait until Genni came out of this faint, Blaine vowed. They were going home. And by home he meant Jubilee. He would kidnap Genni if he had to.

While Blaine waited for them a tall powerful figure, with Genni light as thistledown in his arms, long silk skirt cascading to the floor, they came.

Angel first, looking all of a sudden, years older. Colin, the bridegroom, followed by his best man, both looking utterly bewildered as if they didn't understand what was going on. The bridegroom's parents, George and Victoria Garrett, George huffing and puffing, shaking his bald head in disbelief, the mother looking like she was going to ask for the engagement ring back. Some of the guests collapsing against one another murmuring who knows what? Some looking helplessly over their shoulders as if the person behind them could explain exactly what was happening; some full of concern and sympathy, others cynically pondering the possible reason for the faint. The bridesmaids darted desperate looks at one another. Genevieve gradually came to, knowing on this day at least she wasn't about to say, "I do!"

On doctor's orders the ceremony was "postponed." Doctor Marc Courtland, trapped by the fiercely commanding look in his cousin Blaine's eyes, shook his head ruefully. "Nervous exhaustion" was the diagnosis. The bride obviously needed complete rest.

No one could stop the flood of speculation. With so many guests all dressed up with nowhere to go, it was decided at least the food and drink had to be consumed. With Genevieve tucked away in a very private room in a very expensive private hospital. Angel who had always lived in an operatic lifestyle invited everyone who wished to come back to the house to do so. An astonishing number of people took advantage of her hospitality, desperate to talk about it all—someone must have some dramatic revelations to divulge—and see inside Angel's mansion, which was said to be pretty extravagant.

The Garretts, not surprisingly, disappeared into the night, George Garrett looking very much like the deal was off, while most of the guests pressed ahead famished for food and gossip.

The groom, after he returned from a brief visit to the hospital where he was allowed only a few words with his paper-white would-be bride, was later seen dancing with one of the bridesmaids, apparently not worried about the cataclysmic events of the afternoon or what certain people had plunged into whispering like some soap opera: the bride was really in love with her cousin, Blaine Courtland, the man who was supposed to have given her away. The extraordinary thing was, no one seemed to condemn him. In fact everyone, including the bridegroom, appeared to think him the better man.

If that were true, and at least twenty or more guests, including the bride's mother and the head bridesmaid didn't register amazement, how had it all come to pass? Love was such a force, what complexities of life had brought Genevieve and Blaine to that point?

To understand one would have to go back....

CHAPTER THREE

The Lead-Up

IT HAD been a wonderful day all 'round. A day of high heat and shimmering mirage, capped off by a late afternoon dust storm that blew in from the desert, covering them all with billowing clouds of red dust.

Midmorning one of the mustering crew had come off his motorbike, broken a leg and cracked a few ribs. Soon after, he got the perturbing news the new jackeroo, a kid called Marshall, had been bitten by a desert taipan in the gidgee scrub out at Camp Moggill. No accident, the kid had been fool enough to pick the snake up. Showing off.

God! He could scarcely believe it. And the bloody thing had hung on, its fangs embedded in the boy's arm. He'd had to dash the snake's brains out before he could administer what the station had left of the antivenene. Just a couple of life-saving vials. At that time the kid was barely conscious, muttering over and over he was a total drongo. He couldn't disagree with that.

He'd got off an emergency call to the Flying Doctor posthaste, getting both victims to the station airstrip while they waited for the Super King Air to fly in. Bob Carlin, a great bloke and a fine doctor, had given the boy another shot to be on the safe side. Clarry's leg they'd already set in splints but it needed to be X-rayed.

What might be called a true-blue day. He was desperate for a bath and an ice-cold beer. He could almost feel the tingle in his mouth; nevertheless he worked on tirelessly, not arriving back at the homestead until well after a burning red sun had gone down so slowly it might have been stuck in the sky. A sure sign they'd have more of the same tomorrow.

He entered the house through the back way, not wanting to scatter red dust as he went. The light was on in Lally's room so he made his way down the rear hallway to say hello. Lally was his maiden aunt, Eulalia Courtland, his father's sister. She had come to them after his mother had run off, staying on until his father rebounded into another marriage less than two years later. After his father's funeral he had invited Lally to return to her former home, an invitation she had accepted with tears in her eyes, and Lally wasn't a woman who cried easily. She had been very good to him. He wasn't a man who forgot. Then, too, Lally unlike his stepmother, Delia, and his stepsister, Hilary, shared his powerful love for the land and the remote cattle station that was the Courtlands' ancestral home. Lally was an Outback person. As was he. As was....

Genni.

For a moment his mouth softened unbelievably despite his current turbulent mood towards her. Old memories returned. Genni. The cutest little kid with all the charm in the world. How in the world had she turned into such a blazing hellcat ready to defy him at every turn? Their wonderful relationship based on mutual loyalty and affection, a wealth of shared interests, had almost overnight turned so tempestuous they spent most of their time goading each other. He was supposed to be tough, not a man to cross, most people painted him that way, yet one slip of a girl could and did continually throw him off balance.

Damn her and her silly romances. The last guy she brought out to the station most likely to irritate him, didn't even know how to saddle up a horse. Genni and her boyfriends! Genni and her dreadful mother, the scatty egocentric Angelica, known as Angel. What a misnomer! All of the family to a man blamed Angel for the tragic early death of her first husband, Stephen Courtland, Genni's father and his own father's favourite cousin though one had been a cattle man and the other had followed his dream of becoming an architect. The dream hadn't lasted long.

"Uncle Steve," a courtesy title, had been just as bad a picker of women as his own father. Both women had brought chaos into their husbands' lives. Both had borne their husbands a child. Him and Genni. At least Angel, retaining custody of Genni, had stuck around. His own mother, Crystelle, had run away and never come back. Boy, oh boy, some mother.

At ten he'd had to learn overnight how to stand on his own two feet. He'd had to learn how to cope with heartbreak. *In silence.* His father hadn't helped him. From the day Crystelle left his father he had cut her out of their lives. Her name was never mentioned.

Not even Lally had dared to go against his father's orders, and Lally was a strong personality in her own right. Though she didn't know much about children, with few inbuilt maternal skills, Lally had tried. He was closer to her—the Courtland blood—than he had ever been to Delia who, too, had tried to win his boyish affection but failed. He blamed himself. After his mother's desertion he couldn't seem to open his heart to any strange women. Lally was family. She spoke his language. Delia, pretty, softly spoken, kindly and well meaning as she was to this day, he'd regarded and treated as a stranger for many years. He regretted his cruelty. Delia didn't deserve it. These days they had an easy relationship with little or no friction. It was Genni who had started the thaw on his heart imbuing in him the faith in life destroyed by his mother.

The unforgettable Genni, the little…bitch, he fumed. She certainly had a major talent for exposing his temper.

"Land sakes, you look like a Red Indian!" Lally greeted him, looking up from her book.

"So would you be if you were out in all that dust." He

flashed her a very white smile out of a darkly tanned dust-covered face.

"And how's the boy?" There was concern on Lally's handsome regal face.

"He's learned a powerful lesson. Bob thinks he'll be okay. Clarry went off like the stoic he is."

Lally nodded her agreement, turning away for a moment to pick up a letter from her open bureau. "There's mail for you. Came in on the freight plane."

"I won't read it now." Blaine made to move off. "Just wanted to say hello. I badly need a good scrub. Who's it from, anyway?"

Lally's mouth pursed. "Jinx, would you believe!"

"Probably a sweetly worded request for more money." His grin was cynical.

"I suppose so." Lally gave a deep sigh. "Angel's devotion to money is complete. She's outrageous. Trades on your love for Genni."

He shrugged. "Tell me about it. The only thing is, Genni is not in my good books of late."

Lally reacted swiftly. "Come off it! You're still her hero."

He stared away across the room, his expression regretful. "I was until a few years ago then she got as sassy as all hell."

"Girls, too, like their independence, my boy," Lally reminded him, tucking her glasses into the pocket of her shirt.

"I can't seem to deal with it," he admitted wryly.

His aunt watched him closely. "Well *I* think you're wonderful. Of course, I'm biased, but you're not *perfect*. You've become a bit phobic about Genni, dear. Trying to protect her from everything. She has to learn."

"Not from her mother." Concern soared again in him. "Angel is a bad influence. You've said that yourself. I'd just hate to see Genni follow in Angel's footsteps."

"Well, here now." Lally sat up straight in her armchair,

shaking her silver-grey head vigorously. "Genni is *our* side of the family. She's a far more intelligent, more sensitive and generous person than Angelica could ever be. Angel really only lives for herself."

"I know that," Blaine said, looking a mite dispirited, "but Angel encourages Genni to mix with the wrong people. She has the wrong expectations for her. Hell, Genni wouldn't have gone to university only for me. Angel was going to pack her off to New York, launch her into the modelling world."

"That wouldn't have happened, Blaine," Lally soothed. "Genni didn't want it despite her mother's all-out campaign. In many ways Angel is unstoppable. But Genni has her father's artistic nature. I believe she'll make a fine painter one day."

"I agree. She's pretty damned good now." Blaine exhaled an impatient sigh. "Genni should be concentrating on that aspect of her life instead of running around with a string of lightweight boyfriends. God, I'm really worried Angel will try to marry her off to some rich moron. After all, money is the only thing that counts with Angel."

"Indeed it is. She's obsessed with it, as we know. But there's one important difference, my dear. Money is not the most important thing in the world to Genni. She'll never marry a man she doesn't love."

"Marry?" For a moment Blaine slumped heavily against the doorjamb, rangy body suddenly showing signs of weariness. "Genni needs a lot more living, a lot more maturity before she decides to take on a husband. Hell, the very idea!" He sounded outraged.

"At least you're taking picking the right mate very seriously," Lally said slyly.

He looked at her lazily, then gave her his beautiful smile, a smile that was impossible to resist. "*Don't*, Lally! The thought of marriage brings on a major depression. Who would put up with me?"

Lally snapped her fingers. "Any young woman you asked. You're almost shockingly handsome. You have a fine respected name. You're a dynamo like your father. It has to be said you're not nice and sweet all the time, especially around Genni, but you sure pack an aura."

He straightened from the doorway immediately. "Catch you next time!"

"I'm not saying I object to your lack of vanity," Lally called after him. "Go on, have your bath. Angel's letter will keep."

He finally got 'round to reading it before he went down to dinner. Just Lally and him. Delia and Hilary were having one of their many holidays away, this time in Indonesia, Central Java, to visit the ninth-century Buddhist stupa of Borobudar, the largest Buddhist monument in the world.

"A spiritual journey to enlightenment," Hilary had called it. He hoped it would have some effect on her. His young stepsister, spoiled and overindulged in many respects by her mother, had some kind of inner vulnerability that forever made her feel unloved and insecure.

Ever since he could remember, Hilary had always been in jealous competition. First for their father's love, then when their father had died three years back after suffering a terrible spinal injury out on muster, Hilary had turned her attentions to him. Whenever Genevieve had come to visit there had always been lots of screaming and yelling from Hilary as her somewhat morbid fixations became more intense. The two girls could have been friends. Genni certainly tried. Even Hilary had to acknowledge that, but they never did get on. The reason was obvious to everyone. Hilary had to be first in her father's then her brother's affections so anyone else she perceived got in the way was viewed with antipathy and resentment.

Delia who had done practically everything in her power to remedy matters before turning to over-compensating, al-

ways insisted Hilary would grow out of it. So far Hilary
hadn't, and she was going on nineteen. No great age, he
realized, too, which was what made him so patient with her
and he wasn't patient by nature, what Hilary believed was
actually *true*.

Both he and his father had treated Genni as though she
was more a part of them than their own flesh and blood. But
Genni had made it so easy. Herself deprived of her much
loved father with a mother who always put herself first,
Genni had never vyed for attention, emotionally or any other
way. Naturally sunny-natured, known for her childhood ad-
oration of him, such things had made friendship between the
two girls impossible. One day when Hilary was happily married with a family of her own—his fondest wish come true—
he hoped she would leave all her insecurities behind.
Meanwhile Hilary had a real talent for causing problems.

At least he got the reason for Angel's letter right. As usual
she was after a loan—he had no record of her ever repaying
anything—she didn't know where her money went—unless
it was keeping herself and Genni well dressed. Angel wasn't
close to a con woman, he thought darkly. She was. He knew
for a fact Angel rarely bought Genni anything. Genni from
the first week she started work had paid her own way. He'd
certainly bought Genni a car for her seventeenth then her
twenty-first birthday, the BMW she looked after like a baby.
Jewellery from time to time, seeing Angel couldn't be per-
suaded to part with any of hers.

Angel, meanwhile in between husbands, sent along all the
bills she couldn't handle. Most he paid. Ones in connection
with the house, maintenance, rates, improvements—after all,
Genni lived at home—some he knocked back, antique deal-
ers in particular. They had to see Angel coming. Jubilee
homestead was considered rather grand but it paled in com-
parison to Angel's over the top mansion paid for with
Courtland money.

At the bottom of the letter by way of a P.S. would Blaine

"darling" mind if she brought her current beau, a guy called Slocombe to the annual Polo Ball, this year to be hosted by Jubilee. He had no objection so long as Genni tagged along.

Maybe it would be one of those nights when there was a blissful lack of tension between them. One when Genni would show less provocation and he more tolerance. He had never got to the point when he had seriously considered turning her over his knee, but…! For someone who looked like she did, she had unearthed all manner of turbulent emotions in him. Some he kept tightly canned as though even thinking them was unforgivable. Genni was family! The adorable little girl child with the big violet eyes, white-gold ringlets. The bright star in his life. The prospect of losing sight of that thoroughly unnerved him.

Delia and Hilary arrived home at the end of the following week, physically tired but full of the wonders of their pilgrimage. Indeed Hilary was so inspired she went so far as to announce to a family—who wanted for nothing more— she had achieved "a purer higher state of mind." A claim almost immediately knocked out of the water when Lally told them over a specially prepared delicious three-course dinner, Genni and her mother, as well as her mother's current boyfriend, would be coming to the Polo Ball, which was only a fortnight off.

Hilary exhaled sharply, a gasp of classic outrage. The peaceful expression on her pretty, golden-skinned face was instantly transformed into the sort of storminess that had nearly defeated them all. "The story of my life," she cried hotly, knife and fork frozen in midair. "I get myself a fabulous new dress, I watch my diet the whole time we're away just so I can fit into it, and Genni has to turn up to outshine us all. I really shouldn't have bothered." Now she banged the silverware down.

Blaine, who had had a very hard day, even allowing for his extraordinary recuperative powers, was fed up. "That'll do," he said crisply. "Seems to me you haven't changed a great deal, despite the grand trek. When are you going to give up this tiresome jealousy of Genni? We're all getting sick and tired of trying to humour you. You're your own person with your own special qualities. You must see a pretty girl when you look in the mirror. The way you carry on anyone would think you were downright ugly."

"I swear I am," Hilary burst out, her dark eyes flashing dramatically.

Delia, sitting opposite her, sought as always to appease the daughter who was beginning to quite intimidate her. "No, no, darling," she smiled comfortingly, "you're really lovely. You *are*. Your dress is so beautiful you're going to look ravishing."

"I'm not," Hilary said even more gruffly, sweeping her short glossy brown bangs from her forehead. "Genni makes a positive practice of putting me in the shade."

Lally who didn't interfere often was driven to speak up.

"Genni does no such thing!" she said emphatically in her well-bred voice.

"The new woman!" Blaine saluted his stepsister ironically.

High colour mottled Hilary's cheeks as she flashed Lally a glance like a small poison dart. "All I'm saying is can't Genni stay home for once? And that batty Angel? Every time she opens her mouth I want to strangle her. And her boyfriend. I bet he's horrible. Filthy rich and terrible vulgar. Why don't they just stay away for once?"

"Because I invited them," Blaine responded, quite patiently for him. "If you weren't such a grouch you'd notice Angel adds quite a lot of sparkle to these occasions. Every head turns when she walks in the door. She has the full measure when it comes to glamour."

"And she can be very funny," Delia timidly offered. There was a lot to be said for being funny.

"Never more than when she isn't aware of it," Blaine delicately mocked.

"She's a *hex!*" Hilary tilted her small freckled nose into the air. "She's not an Angel, either. Far from it." Hilary was well into her stride, wanting to claw and slash whenever Genni's name was mentioned. "Genni is the angelic-looking one. So beautiful and bright and innocent. *Innocent? Why* she's as sexy as they come. I bet she's no virgin, either. Not with all those boyfriends hanging 'round her."

Blaine, at the head of the gleaming mahogany table, suddenly squared his wide shoulders, fixing Hilary with a diamond-hard glance. "It's not often I've sent you from the table, Hilary. After all, you're supposed to be an adult. But you can excuse yourself right now."

At the forcefulness of his tone an expression of real fright touched Hilary's dark eyes. She rose so awkwardly she sent her long-stemmed wineglass, which only contained mineral water, over. "That's right. Go on," she flounced, furious tears springing into her eyes. "You should have been Genni's Black Knight. So you can defend her to the death."

As Delia was officially mistress of Jubilee Downs, the planning and organization of the Polo Weekend and the culminating Gala Ball should have fallen to her, but such were her lack of organisational skills and interest in a game that excited great Outback passions; a game at which her late husband and her stepson excelled, since her return to her family home, Lally had taken all responsibility out of Delia's grateful hands. The result was whenever it was Jubilee's turn to hold meets and ultimately if their team won the Gala Ball, everything went exceedingly well. Nevertheless Lally, who wasn't getting any younger, and the number of people, teams and spectators who attended, always getting larger, she was very appreciative of Genni's offer to help.

Genni was very methodical, like herself. She undertook whatever she had to do with great care and energy. Lally never had to tell her the same thing twice. She had grown up with it, soaking up the whole exciting atmosphere like a sponge. It made up somehow for the disappointment Lally felt at Delia's and her young niece's lack of excitement in the event, although Hilary since she had grown up looked forward to the ball.

Delia, on the other hand, was shy by nature. She didn't feel comfortable with crowds of people. She found it difficult to make small talk with people she didn't know. She was the complete opposite of Blaine's beautiful mother, Crystelle. The very reason my poor brother married her, Lally thought. Crystelle, beautiful, brilliant, had fled him, unable to cope with the isolation of station life. Delia, quiet and retiring, was a woman who could be counted on to stay put. Lally had grown genuinely fond of Delia but she deplored Delia's lack of parental control over her mercurial daughter.

Hilary's tantrums were becoming increasingly exhausting although she had been on her best behaviour since Blaine had so clearly shown his displeasure. Hilary had gone down to the station airstrip to welcome Angel's party when they flew in. She had greeted Angel and Genni with a rare peck on the cheek, been respectful to Toby Slocombe, a big, slightly overweight man with a very nice smile and shrewd intelligent eyes, and somewhat flirtatious with Genni's beau, Colin Garrett of the soft floppy hair and crinkling hazel eyes. Genni had asked and been given permission to bring him. Lally only hoped the pleasantness would last.

"It must have taken a lot of work to keep the grass so green and velvety in the heat," Genni's musical voice broke into Lally's thoughts. They were working in the utility room of the kitchen, finishing off the flower arrangements.

Lally nodded with satisfaction. "I got the boys to follow Blaine's advice." When Blaine had time, he was around to supervise. "I worry about Blaine. He works too hard." Lally stood back to admire a huge Chinese vase she had filled with soaring branches of white bauhinia. The orchid-like flowers would fall soon enough but for a day or two the arrangement would look magical. "The going can't be too tough, as we know," she continued. "Can't jar the ponies legs. On the other hand if the turf is too soft it will slow them down. Where's your boyfriend, by the way?"

"He's deserted me for Blaine." Genni smiled. "Blaine has that effect on people. The last time I saw them Blaine was showing Colin and Toby around the field, explaining things to them, I expect. Neither of them knows the game. Afterwards he was going to take them down to the stables to see the ponies. You've done a wonderful job, Lally." Genni slipped her arm around the older woman, momentarily leaning her ash-blond head affectionately against Lally's. "I've missed you."

"I've missed you, too, girl." Lally not terribly used to physical demonstrations of affection spoke a little stiffly, but her regal face wore a poignant expression, a combination of pleasure and sadness, perhaps at her own childless state. "Do you like all the flags I've put up around the grounds?" she asked, clearing her throat slightly.

"They look great." Genni, understanding Lally very well, went back to her own work. "So does the new way you've placed all the tables and chairs under the trees. It looks like an al fresco restaurant. The Great Hall looks marvellous, too. You must have been very very busy, especially with Delia and Hilary away."

"I'm glad of something to do," Lally confided. "I changed my mind a couple of times about the decoration of the hall. Sure you like it?"

"Of course I do." Genni smiled encouragement. "You have great taste, Lally. It's all so wonderfully exciting, isn't it? Colin's over the moon. He's never been outback before. He loves everything he sees."

"Is it serious with Colin?" Lally asked, inwardly shying away from a "yes" answer.

"We're fairly close. I'm just enjoying myself, Lally,"

Genni answered blithely. "Colin is very easy to be with. He's a lot of fun and he knows how to get around Angel."

"What man doesn't?" Lally snorted, tucking a stray silver-grey lock back into the easy French pleat she had worn for years now.

"Don't be naughty," Genni scolded her, waving a forefinger.

"And Mr. Slocombe?" Lally flipped Genni a sparkling glance.

"Aaah! Now that *could* be serious." Genni dropped her head owlishly. "At least Angel is hoping so."

"She's likely to have as many husbands as Elizabeth Taylor," Lally, husbandless, offered dryly, but not without a certain small envy.

"Oh, don't say that!" Genni implored. "I'm having trouble keeping up as it is. Actually Angel introduced Colin to me. I think you could safely say she's given him the thumbs up. His father is George Garrett. You know, the Freight King?" Genni stopped to get Lally's attention.

Lally looked back dry as ash. "I guessed as much. Don't let your mother push you into anything you don't want, darling girl. She's good at that. A born manipulator."

"She only wants the best for me, Lally." Genni shook her head, ever loyal. "At least in her own way. She hasn't really grasped we're completely different. Neither for that matter has Blaine."

Lally stopped what she was doing, anxious to get her message across. "Now take it easy with Blaine this weekend, hear? He has enough to put up with with young Hilary."

"Lally, dearest, I'm going to do my level best. As for Hilary, she'll settle down given enough time. Life here is too remote for her. She's not a bush person."

"She really doesn't have anything of her father in her." Lally clicked her tongue. "Just between the two of us," Lally leaned closer, "Delia lets her get away with murder."

"An only child?" Genni excused, cautiously.

"What are you two whispering about?" a familiar male voice demanded from the doorway. A dark-timbered voice that caused a rush of goose bumps down Genni's arms.

She swung her blond head, caught at the nape with a deep blue ribbon. She had a sudden irresistible urge to reach out and hug him like she used to, instead she said casually, "Hi!"

"Hi yourself?" His beautiful smile flashed over her as he moved into the room with his characteristic easy grace. A plain white T-shirt stretched over his wide taut chest, beautiful muscular forearms, tight-fitting blue jeans, lean, long flanks. Sexy as hell. "Missed you at breakfast."

"I went for a ride." She didn't say she'd hoped to catch up with him. "Didn't anyone tell you?"

"Actually Lollypop did the moment I walked into the stables." Lollypop was the part aboriginal stable hand so called because of his habit of always juggling a lollypop in his mouth. "He also told me you took The Boxer?"

"That's okay, isn't it?" She spoke sweetly, mindful of Lally's request.

"I don't know." Blaine rubbed his cleft chin, his good-health skin gleaming in the golden light from the open windows. "He's proving a bit tricky. I think I'll have to have him gelded. I know you're a good rider, having taught you *very well*—" he exaggerated "—myself, but I'd prefer it if you stuck with Aurora for this visit. Okay?"

She moved nearer to him to sketch a little series of Arabian gestures. "Your wish is my command," she murmured submissively.

"Really?"

For a moment it seemed to Genni he was gazing right *into* her, so unaccountably she flushed. "Absolutely."

"I intend to remind you of that one of these days, violet eyes." Languidly he leaned over and tugged one of her curls.

"I have complete confidence you will. So where did you leave Colin and Toby?"

"Ah, Colin and Toby! The boyfriends!" His silver glance was mocking. "I'm sure I remember them."

"I assure you they're very impressed with you. And your style of living."

"You wouldn't lie to me, would you, Genni?" Another half smile, his teeth superbly white. "Anyway, Toby couldn't have gone more than a minute before Angel came looking for him. I let Colin have one of the Jeeps. He wants to take a look around but he's promised not go out too far. I don't want to have to go looking for him."

She turned her slender body to stare directly at him. "Are you sure?"

"What are you accusing me of?" he challenged. "Of course I'm sure. I make it my business to look after your boyfriends."

"Oh-ho and what about Josh Hamilton?" This time her tone was tart.

"Don't remember the name." His laugh was low but far from gentle. "These arrangements are really beautiful." He walked about, looking at what they'd done. "I especially like this." He dipped his dark head to smell the ravishing fragrance of a mix of summer flowers, his mouth almost touching a rose petal. For some reason Genni's heart contracted. Blaine could be so damned…erotic at times. Or so it struck her.

"Genni's work," Lally told him with pride. "She's an artistic genius."

"You and me both!" Genni, putting an arm around Lally's trim waist, embraced her. "You know the lovely life-size marble lady in the entrance hall, I thought I'd place this arrangement in her hand?" She looked to Blaine for his opinion, indicating a charming small arrangement of yellow roses, butter-yellow ranunculus, little sprigs of wattle with touches of green.

"Why not? A lady should constantly receive flowers from an admirer. Let me do it." He glanced at Lally and smiled. "I guess I'll be horrified at the bill?"

"Comfort yourself, my dear, a surprising amount came from the home gardens. I've had Fred and his helpers working hard. The rest, the more delicate blooms, all the blues and mauves and lilacs were flown in. We've had them in the cold room."

"So where's Hilary?" He cocked a brow. "I asked her to give you a hand."

"That's okay. Genni and I managed."

"Brilliantly by the look of it." Blaine glanced in Genni's direction. "I'm on my way over to the Great Hall. Do you want to come?"

"Sure. Lally can't handle positioning all these vases, though."

"We're not going to ask her. I'll do it before we go."

"Listen you two," Lally clucked fondly, so much wanting them to spend time together, "I've got Ruby and the girls to help me." She referred to Jubilee's long-time housekeeper and her small well-trained domestic staff. "So leave. Go enjoy yourselves and remember what I told you, Genni."

"Yes, Lally dearest!" Genni gave her a cheeky wave from the door.

So like her mother. So unlike her mother. Stephen was there too, Lally thought.

Moments later they were out in the hot sunshine, walking away from the magnificent double-storied homestead with its balconies and pillared verandas and cast-iron lace balustrade, towards what the family called the Great Hall, a multi-purpose building used for meetings, cattle conventions, family weddings, balls and parties, even a glamorous show ring to show off the highly sought-after polo ponies bred by the station and offered at packed sales.

"So what did Lally tell you?" Blaine questioned, glancing down at Genni's lovely tranquil profile.

"A secret!" She put a finger to her lips, almost dancing to keep up with his long stride.

"Some secret. I bet she told you to be sweet to me."

"I mean to be." She gave him a provocative little smirk.

"And no one sweeter when you choose."

"That goes for you, too." She smiled at him in a way even she didn't realize. "I love you when you're not up on your high horse. So what do you think of Colin? Tell me, I'm dying to know."

He gave a mock yawn. "Who?"

"Pleeze!" She angled a mocking glance.

He laughed shortly. "Likeable. Nice manners. Certainly an improvement on some of the others."

"In case you're interested, it's not serious." So why had she said that when she and Colin had been an item for months now? She didn't want to know.

"I wasn't thinking he was your lover?" Blaine's down-bent glance was so searing it burned.

"Listen. I don't think you'd approve of anyone I wanted to marry?" she challenged, realising in some confusion she couldn't bear to think of Sally Fenwick as Blaine's future bride, either.

"I guess I've played the role of Big Brother for too long," Blaine murmured, his voice a shade metallic.

"Anyway, Colin is just a friend. For now." Her heart was pumping like she was telling lies.

"I'll take your word for it."

She flickered a glance at him. He was so absolutely beautiful to her, like some godlike creature. "Oh, let's be friends!" She grasped his arm in an excess of brittle joy, hugging it the way she used to. "I've so been looking forward to this weekend."

"Me, too," he murmured, but his expression was unreadable.

*   *   *

They were almost at the hall when the sound of an approaching aircraft resonated in the air. "Another plane coming in." Genni turned her head skywards as the light aircraft began to circle the homestead on its way to the station airstrip. Light aircraft carrying guests had been landing all morning, dotting the fields to either side. "Do I know them?"

Blaine shaded his eyes. "Sure you do. That's the Camerons. I expect they're all travelling together."

"Great. It's been a long time. Oh, goodness!" Genni broke off lowering her head protectively as a strong breeze blew down the canyon of the outbuildings, catching her ribbon, tugging it from her hair as debris blew into her eye.

She moaned.

"Oh, hell!" Instantly Blaine turned her the other way, sheltering her with his body, while the air settled down.

"There's something in my eye."

"Here, let me. No, don't rub it in." He drew her beneath a broad awning, pulling a handkerchief out of his jeans' pocket. "This is perfectly clean. Stand still, cherub. Lift your head. Look at me."

"I can't." She blinked, dreading the notion she might have a red eye for the party.

"Be brave." There was a smile in his voice.

"Oh, go on then." Genni held up her face, widening her eyes, the tip of her pink tongue pressed against her bowed upper lip to assist her concentration.

Deftly Blaine twisted his white handkerchief into a little peak, gently foraging for the dark speck. "I've got it!" he announced with considerable satisfaction, looking down at her when inexplicably his whole body turned as taut as piano wire. She could feel the abrupt change through his hand.

What was up?

Genni held her position for a moment while she blinked several times. "That's better." She opened her eyes to smile up at him only to encounter a gaze so full of strange glittering lights she was dazzled, unnerved. "Blaine?" Her voice wobbled, as tremulous as a child's.

There was a sharp, very difficult pause. A moment of revelation so potent it was almost a terror. Every pulse in her body quickened. She couldn't look away yet they stood in this ongoing radiant white silence, until Blaine reached out and put his hands on her slender hips and drew her towards him. On this day of days there were people all over the station yet the whole world emptied to just the two of them. Hushed.

"You want me to tell you something?" she whispered, trembling and shaking. "You can be very frightening at times."

"Like now?"

She almost sank to her knees in shock. The Blaine she knew had assumed another shape, so powerful, so intoxicating it was like being taken over. Possessed. A pulse beat wildly in her throat. Her small breasts rose steeply beneath her silk shirt. Sexual sensations were whispering and humming all over her skin like little currents of electricity, drawing a small moan to her lips. "What are you doing?" Her violet eyes darkened, a flush like crushed rose petals stained her cheeks.

Doing? God, he was as shaken as she was, but hiding it much better. He knew he should stop. She wasn't ready for this but his own will was dissolving under a weight of tenderness and a tremendous rush of desire that clouded his judgment. This was Genni. She was forbidden to him. Which was total rubbish. Then again, he wasn't feeling rational. Her breath smelled of apples, sweet and fresh. The tip of her tongue was a leaf around which his own ached to twine.

She was so beautiful. So desperately beautiful, the substance of dreams, with her masses of white-gold hair cascading around her shoulders and down her back, those violet eyes imploring him not to risk altering everything in a minute. Their whole relationship.

He could see her little convulsive swallows but that didn't stop him arching her imperceptibly closer. How pliant was her slender body. How delicately executed. He wanted to bring up a hand, slip a pearly button on the pale silk of her beautiful shirt. He wanted to expose a small exquisite breast, bring his mouth to the tightly budded nipple, so clearly betraying; peaked against the gossamer-light material. She was looking back at him tortured, bewitched, her self-possession all gone. He wanted to kiss her open-mouthed. All the kisses they had exchanged over the years. Scattered pecks. Sometimes tight little extravagant smacks when she arrived. "Home sweet home!"

This kiss would be different. Unlike any kiss she had ever received before in her life. He would fold his mouth over hers, finding it as lush and pulsing as ever a man dreamed of, pressing down harder...deeper and deeper, drinking her in as if from a glistening life-giving spring.

God help him, he wanted her so badly in a moment he would haul her to him. Pick her up. Carry her away, Precious Genni. Her power over him was spellbinding.

Unsuspecting of the scene that was unravelling, Hilary and Sally Fenwick in tow rounded a corner, they, too, on their way to the Great Hall. Their jaws fell open to see Genni standing perfectly still under Blaine's hands, yet poised like a creature too mesmerized to take flight. Blaine's gleaming black head was bent over her in an attitude so intense, so sexual it was like the two of them were enveloped in clouds of smoke.

"Oh, great heavens!" poor Sally cried, feeling seared to the bone, but unable to look away. "Let's go back," she begged, clutching at Hilary's hand.

"Don't be silly." Hilary gave a small dangerous smile. "Don't you know Genni does this all the time?"

"Does what?" Sally's halting voice shook. She had always liked Genni. They got on extremely well.

"Genni loves playing these little flirting games," Hilary explained, making no attempt to hide her disgust. "She's like her mother. It doesn't mean anything. She's as good as engaged to the guy she brought with her."

"Is she?" Sally who'd adored Blaine Courtland for most of her life and really felt she had a chance with him, forced some air into her depleted lungs. "If you ask me it's Genni who should be protected."

"From whom?" Hilary snapped, in her own private hell.

"Why...Blaine. He looks like he's about to drag her off like a caveman. He never looks like that with me."

"You don't understand Blaine," Hilary responded grimly. "He has to be lord and master. What you're seeing doesn't mean *a thing*. You're the girl Blaine has in his sights. Genni is family."

It was far from Sally's conclusion. Not now. What she had understood to be their relationship—cousins—had been brutally swept aside. They looked like lovers. Sally couldn't really comprehend it. She felt shell-shocked.

The two teams cantered out onto the field to thunderous high-spirited cheers that circled and rose into the clear desert air to startle the birds. Four men to a team, wearing the traditional helmet, jersey, snowy-white breeches, high glossy-black boots. The championship had already been won by Blaine's team, the impressive silver cup displayed on the library table in the homestead's entrance hall. This was an exhibition match to add to the excitement and unashamed glamour of the weekend.

For the first chukka, Blaine was riding a magnificent chestnut gelding whose hide gleamed like satin in the brilliant sunshine. His team wore a distinctive red-and-black jersey piped with white; the opposition, emerald-green and navy.

Genni couldn't look away from Blaine though she had seen him playing countless times. He looked magnificent in the saddle, a veritable paragon of masculine dash and daring. Quick thinking, physically and mentally tough with all the shots, this had earned him his usual position as Number Two. His job as the most influential attacking player, to work closely with his Number One, the front player, keeping the ball moving up the field which today thanks to a lot of hard work looked velvety green. They were playing a full match divided into six seven-minute chukkas. Each player needed a string of ponies, at least three, as no pony due to the rigorous demands of the game was ever used for more than two consecutive chukkas. It was this that made the game so expensive to play.

"Gosh, these guys are really something!" Colin raised his brows and whistled, turning to smile at Genni, who was reclining comfortable in a deck chair. They had found a deliciously cool spot beneath the trees, their gourmet hamper to one side, a bottle of champers on ice. "Why didn't you tell me your cousin was such a glamorous character?" he chortled, quite without envy. One of the nicest things about him. "You don't see guys like that all that often. Hell, he looks like a film star playing a polo player in a movie. And would you listen to all those females shrieking his name."

"He doesn't hear them, believe me," Genni offered very dryly, knowing it to be true.

"It'd go right to my head," Colin freely admitted, taking a gulp of eucalypt fragrant air. "Say, this is the life! A gorgeous girl, champers, hampers and a jolly good game of polo." He tried his best pukka accent. "Never thought I'd enjoy myself so much. It must be a powerful thing to rule over your own kingdom. Which as far as I can see is pretty much what your cousin does."

Genni's eyes were shaded by her designer sunglasses. "He takes the job very seriously, Colin. Jubilee, like the other famous stations, is our pioneering history."

"Yes, indeed! I had to see it to believe it!" Colin was thoroughly enjoying himself. "And that homestead! They sure know how to live. He's a wonderful rider. I expect he'd have to be born in the saddle."

"True but they don't all ride so elegantly. You'll see just how good Blaine is when they start to play. Blaine and his horse move as one. The accord between man and pony is total. It doesn't happen overnight. Blaine puts a lot of his time into training his ponies. It takes a lot of work."

"They don't look like ponies to me." Colin's eyes surveyed the teams' mounts. "They look more like they belong at the races."

"Blaine's mount is a thoroughbred. So are most of the others. A couple of three-quarter thoroughbreds.

"Polo mounts are always referred to as ponies," Genni explained. "Pony is just a term. Blaine reads the game better than most. He's a great one for tactics." On and off the field, she thought with a pang of the heart. "That's what won them the cup. Both teams were excellent but Blaine brought the better tactics to bear."

"What's the big sigh for?" Colin turned to her in surprise. "It sounded like it came from deep inside you."

"Oh, sometimes Blaine can be overwhelming," Genni found herself confessing.

Colin considered briefly. "I can see that. He's been very nice to me, though."

"He likes you."

"Great!" Colin's attractive grin lit up his face. "I'm damned sure you and I won't be going places unless we have your cousin onside." Colin reached out and took Genni's hand, carrying it to his lips. "You look good enough to eat. A delicious strawberry-and-vanilla gelato."

Genni was wearing linen pants with a matching sleeveless shirt in a vivid shade of pink, her head and her eyes protected by a large floppy hat in finest cream straw, the brim decorated with pink full-blown roses.

"Mmm!" He began to lick the back of her hand. "What are you wearing tonight? Something seriously sexy I hope?"

"Collette Dinnigan. Your only clue."

"That's enough!" Colin smiled broadly, then lay back. "I just love a woman to look like a woman. Appealing but revealing. You do things to me, Genni, no one has ever done before. I love being with you. I'm beginning to think I need to be with you all the time."

Exhibition game or not the match was played at a furious pace, individual daring bringing the heart into the throat. At half-time, with the goals equal, Genni stayed well back, not going up to Blaine to have a word as she had done for years but watching proceedings from her leafy shelter beneath the trees.

Blaine was busy changing his jersey, unconsciously displaying his great physical shape still not registering the oohs and aahs and burst of girlish giggles around the field.

Colin had gone off to speak to one of the spectators he recognised from back in his college days, so she was able to sit quietly trying to understand what had happened only a few short hours before. Whatever it was it amounted to a crisis point. The world around her had changed. Even Colin. She thought she was in love with him. Or love as she had understood it. Now she was horribly confused.

Ignorance is bliss.

Across the field she saw Sally Fenwick, even at a distance flushed with pleasure, tall and athletic in very trendy dress-up denim go up to Blaine, put her arms around him and kiss his cheek. Perhaps a lot more shyly than Sally usually did. But then Sally and Hilary had witnessed that odd scene outside the Great Hall where hers and Blaine's emotions had inexplicably got out of hand. Blaine had been sufficiently in control of himself to recover in a moment, but she had continued to stand there in a daze, as Sally and Hilary continued down the walkway to join them.

Hilary's dark eyes had flashed the usual getting-to-be-boring message, "I hate you!" Sally, who was really very nice, had tried her familiar friendly smile but underneath Genni knew she was stricken. As well she might be. Sally had hung in there far longer than any of the others. Sally knew what she wanted out of life. That want was Blaine Courtland.

Play was due to start again. Colin returned, coming up behind her, laying his hands possessively on her shoulders. "Miss me, darling?"

"No, not at all!" She gave him a backward smile. "You were only gone ten minutes."

"If you loved me that's long enough, you know." Colin, his clean shiny hair flopping onto his forehead, bent over her, dropping a lingering kiss on her mouth.

All of which was noticed on and around the field.

CHAPTER FOUR

The Polo Ball

CLOUDLESS heavens. A billion glittering desert stars. The Milky Way a jewel-encrusted ribbon. Over the homestead roof. The Southern Cross, the Guiding One, in all its unique magic.

Inside the house there was still a huge crowd although the ball was already under way, the sound of the band's music carrying strongly on the night air.

Blaine made his way through the whirling crowd, submitting to one fervent embrace after the other. Lots of cooing. Arms flung wide in greeting.

"Blaine, daaarling, you've been ignoring me!"

"Blaine, promise you're going to dance with me!"

"Daaarling Blaine, you look simply divine in evening clothes!"

Wafts of expensive perfume, pretty mouths, pretty teeth, colourful rustling dresses. What man in his right mind would object to being pounded on by a bevy of very attractive young women who left him in no doubt of their feelings. All of them his for the asking. It filled him with no sense of triumph. Only a kind of bittersweet longing for that one woman he knew could fill his heart.

With practised sardonic charm Blaine made his way through the main reception rooms, gratified the homestead was looking its very best, all the while wondering where Genni was. Genni unlike her mother had never been one for staging an entrance. She should be down by now. He wanted to direct everyone over to the Great Hall.

He had barely reached the entrance hall when he heard a male voice call out, There's Genni!'' There was so much delight in the tone, he was searingly conscious he, too, was experiencing an enormous inner quickening.

Genni.

So then he looked up at her.

She was standing at the first landing of the grand curving staircase, her lovely face brilliant in animation, smiling and waving, radiating so perfectly the sheer pleasure and excitement of the evening.

How was it, he wondered, when he had barely noticed what the other women wore he took in every last detail of Genni's appearance? She had her beautiful hair long and loose, the way he liked best, the front caught up in some arrangement adorned with a jewelled clip. Her dress was a beautiful shade of blue, echoing her eyes, the filmy fabric sewn with swirls of the same colour sequins. Here and there full-blown deep pink silk roses were embroidered. He realized the cut was pretty much as revealing as a slip, but much more romantic, a barely there kind of dress with a crossover skirt that showed off one long slender leg and her exquisite evening sandals. His breath caught hard and fast. He felt a powerful tide of pride in her. And possession. This was his Genni. He had always had such joy in her. He wanted to claim her. Shut her away from the sight of any other man. God, it almost amused him he was in such a vulnerable state of mind.

Genni, looking down at the sea of faces, all bright and smiling, suddenly realized she was intent on singling out a particular glinting gaze. Suddenly she saw him. He was standing near the tall double doors that led to the drawing room, a strangely handsome, commanding kind of man.

And there it was again, a recurrence of the afternoon. A look of naked sensuality barely veiled in his upturned silver glance.

Oh, God, she hadn't misread it. Just as she hadn't misread

it hours before. Once again she was left reeling: alarmed and feverishly excited by the impact of a single glance. There was such a thrilling quality about Blaine. A physical exhilaration that on these occasions made her legs go weak and her throat go dry. She knew she was looking back questioningly at him, feeling the heat in her cheeks. Whatever lifetime of affection that had lain between them was being invaded by a powerful sense of something else. What? Genni, heart hammering, felt she had entered another country.

And then he smiled. His rare slow, magical smile that lit his dark face to radiance.

She smiled back. Nope, he only meant he was proud of her. Even as her heartbeats began to settle, and the panic that had washed her started to subside, she felt a profound pang of disappointment. Disappointment at what? At what precise moment had her view of her childhood hero changed? He was still her hero, whether they truly got on or not, but she couldn't begin to wrestle with all these other treacherous emotions that were crowding her, backing her against a brick wall. What had never been could not be. He was toying with her. He had a dark streak.

Genni walked down the thickly carpeted Persian runner marshalling her defences against that all-powerful figure in her life. Her arrogant cousin Blaine. She was still physically dizzy but she held her head high. Not for the first time it occurred to her Blaine was a very dangerous man. And judging from the expressions on the faces of the young women surrounding him her own fascination was echoed over and over. In a word, Blaine was dynamite.

When she reached the lowest step he had made his way through the crowd, who despersed like magic at his approach, to put out a lazy hand. "Now the ball can begin."

His silver eyes still sparkled with something Genni hadn't the courage to name. "You look wonderful," she said, deliberately keeping her voice sweet and cousinly, relieved beyond words it sounded just that.

"You were the prettiest little girl I've ever seen," he drawled. "You still are." It was a near physical kiss. His mouth on hers.

God! A million stars burst inside her. He was wicked! "Part of me loves you." she whispered very softly, leaning her white-gold head in towards him. "The best part. So be agreeable tonight."

"And you behave yourself, as well," he clipped off, lifting her hand to kiss it, ignoring if he even noticed the tremble in her white fingers. He drew her towards the door, calling to everyone to follow them to the Great Hall.

Out on the veranda, Colin came rushing up the short flight of steps, exclaiming as he came, "Genni, baby, I thought you'd never get dressed. I've been waiting for you for ages. You look gorgeous!" Colin closed in on them but Blaine didn't relinquish Genni's arm, the set of his wide shoulders beneath the fine cloth of his dinner jacket and a certain routine imperious expression indicating Colin wasn't going to claim his "girlfriend" for a while. Colin in high good spirits made do by walking alongside, thanking Blaine over and over for being "so darn nice" as to invite him. He was having a whale of a time.

By ten o'clock the ball was in full swing. From the network of beams in the Great Hall with its huge cathedral-like space, hung a spectacular lineup of polo flags of all countries, their bold bright colours lighting up the area. Appended from the lowest beams were great double-sided framed action shots of that year's championships match taken by an Outback photographer who had become internationally famous. One could see why. The photographs were a triumph; so glamorous and romantic. Genni's eye gravitated to them time and time again. She loved the shots featuring Blaine, particularly one that caught him at the precise moment, arm held aloft, when he was preparing to square cut a ball. His chestnut pony's two front legs were well clear of the ground, Blaine's two team-mates had fallen back to give him room for the full free swing that was to score the deciding goal.

"A real winner, isn't it?" Lally, regal in navy lace, a beautiful turquoise and pearl choker 'round her throat turned to Genni, a flush of pleasure on her face at the success of the evening.

"No doubt about it." Warmly Genni slipped an arm through Lally's. "It really takes hold of the imagination. Everyone's having a wonderful time. Isn't that great!"

"I'm so pleased." Lally's fine eyes were twinkling. "Even our little Hilary has been won around, but I think her dress is wrong. I'm not sure why. It's beautiful enough."

"Maybe just a little too sophisticated," Genni said thoughtfully. "But she looks lovely and she's in such a good mood."

"Which she should be all the time of course." Lally's voice sharpened a fraction. "Given how much is done for her."

"There goes Angel!" Genni interrupted, giving her mother a little wave as she and Toby Slocombe boogied past. No old-fashioned fox trots for Angel. She was absolutely up to the minute. She had caused a sensation when she had first appeared in her Chanel couture strapless number with tiers and tiers of ruffles for a skirt, a huge scarlet silk camellia fixed to a white shoulder, a billion-dollar smile on her face.

"Sometimes I think she deserves a twenty-one gun salute," Blaine had quipped at the time.

Now Genni and Lally looked with pleasure around the dance floor. As usual the women had gone to town, grateful for the opportunity to dress up and look beautiful for their men. Every colour of the rainbow was on the floor, pinks, blues, purples, lots of floral patterns and appliqués. Sequins and paillettes caught every turn of the huge revolving disco light, setting the metallic dresses from silver to bronze and glitzy gold to pure dazzle.

Across the room Sally Fenwick, head thrown back, naked back arched, was riding a wave of pleasure locked in Blaine's arms. He must have been saying something amusing because Sally was laughing joyously, the sound coming clearly over the buzz of conversation and the loudness of the band. Whatever he had told her about that odd scene she and Hilary had stumbled on, Sally had been prepared to believe it. Or maybe Hilary had convinced her it had been her fault. Blaine looked relaxed. Probably telling Sally how wonderful she looked, which she did, though her strapless electric blue satin dress was falling perilously low and Sally had an eye-catching full bosom. Not that any man present would take exception to that, Genni thought.

Both women turned as Colin returned, holding the cold drink Genni had requested. Even with all the doors and windows opened, and many fans circling, the crush of people had raised the temperature in the hall.

"Here you are, beautiful." Colin smiled at Genni with great pride and pleasure, thinking how exquisitely beautiful she looked. No wonder his father had congratulated him on winning Genni's affections. He wondered how she would react if he popped the question. Feeling all warm and reckless, Colin still remembered to turn to Lally. "Could I get anything for you, Miss Lally?" he asked courteously, slightly in awe of Miss Eulalia Courtland though she had been very gracious.

"No thank you, my dear." She shook her elegantly coiffured head. "I must see about supper." With a nod and a smile Lally moved off, looking around for a particular friend with whom she wanted to have a word. The ball was in full swing. She thought the first wave for supper should be timed for another half hour. She only hoped the gossip columnist who usually came along to these affairs wouldn't use the word "sumptuous" in connection with the supper, though it undoubtedly was.

"Let's take a whirl, princess," Colin put his arm around

Genni's waist, steering her towards the dance floor. "I need to hold you in my arms."

Genni laughed as she looked up at him. "Do you know you've developed an Outback drawl?"

"Specially for you, darlin'." Colin gathered her in close, revelling in her femininity and the magnificent chaos of white-gold curls that fell over his arm. "This little trip has been marvellous for me. It's settled a lot of things in my mind."

"Like what," Genni said, almost conversationally.

"Like what would marriage be like to a beautiful warm-hearted girl like you?" Colin could feel himself excited as he said it. He even felt a smidgeon of the old familiar panic.

Genni wasn't certain if he was serious or not. "You're not letting this go to your head, are you, Colin? I thought you didn't see yourself as a husband?" Most people perceived Colin Garrett as a playboy.

"Maybe not in the past. But now... I can't give you up." Colin's gaze grew soft and serious. At that moment he believed himself deeply in love. He couldn't remember feeling quite like that before. He had to do something. On a rush of emotion, he bent his head and kissed Genni very lingeringly on the mouth, feeling her lips open like velvety petals. She was perfect to kiss. *Perfect!* It wouldn't be too long before he could get her into bed with him. She hadn't much liked the idea up to date.

"Did you see that?" A distance away, Hilary, standing momentarily with her stepbrother, felt she had been handed a golden opportunity. "Genni has finally fallen in love," she gulped. "I never thought it was going to happen. She loves to play the field."

"Really?" Blaine sounded distant. He followed her gaze, as did most people. "That's a bit of a refrain of yours isn't it, Hilary?" He looked across the swirling sea of celebrating couples to where Colin and Genni were clasped in each other's arms. They appeared to be rocking gently on the spot, apparently oblivious to everyone around them. "It's a fact of life beautiful young women get pursued."

"Oh quite!" Hilary responded in high glee. "Only this time it looks like Colin is going to catch her. Did you ever see two people so totally engaged in each other? Genni told me she was *very* interested." She stared up at Blaine to gauge his reaction, finding his handsome face set in lines of disbelief.

"When did she tell you that? I don't think you've spent more than five minutes together," he scoffed.

"How would you know?" She kept her tone sweet and reasonable. "You weren't around most of the time. You were playing polo. She told me this afternoon after the match."

"They're just friends." Blaine sounded very definite. Too definite for Hilary, who was determined to make mischief.

She grasped her stepbrother's jacketed arm, standing on tiptoes to whisper confidentially, "I can tell you she's working hard to convince you of that. I don't know *why* exactly. She actually warned me to keep quiet. You have to admit she doesn't like you to know what she's up to. You object such a lot. She'll tell you, all right, when it's too late for you to do anything about it. Anyway I like him. And he wants Genni so much. Anyone can see that."

"At least two hundred and fifty people, I'd say." Typically Blaine sounded sardonic.

In the next moment a partner came to claim Hilary and she moved triumphantly out onto the floor. Every chance she got to come between Blaine and Genni she was going to take. She'd lived too many years in the shadow of Genni's glory.

He waited until Colin had left Genni's side for a brief moment before he made his move.

"Is it my imagination or have you been avoiding me?" He closed each of his fingers around her silky bare arm.

"I think I probably have." Feeling as she did she wasn't about to lie.

"Why?" He moved her out onto the dance floor, knowing it was a mistake.

"You damned well know why. You can't blame me." His arms around her made her feel physically weak. So weak it was like some powerful drug had hit her bloodstream. Although she appeared as cool as a lily, inwardly she was swept by a wave of high emotion. She felt like she was standing on a ledge. Unprotected. What game was Blaine playing? She would die of humiliation if he was only trying to prove his control over her. Didn't he know he tore the heart from her?

He held her in silence *for* a few moments, bodies close, Genni feeling so shivery she burst out spontaneously, "I don't know if I can bear this." A dead give-away, but she couldn't control it.

His long arm tightened. "Bear what? Don't even think of trying to make a fool of me, Violetta."

His old nickname for her sparked many complex feelings. "That wouldn't do would it?"

"Not when everybody's having such a good time. Why are you afraid to talk to me?"

He was such a wonderful mover. A natural. He made Colin seem flat-footed. "I'm upset, that's why," she admitted, staring over his shoulder.

"Really, I would have said just the reverse. That little love scene with Garrett was worth watching."

"Maybe he's just the sort of man I need," she answered desperately.

"I can't think how you arrived at that conclusion." His voice was coolly level. "Although I have to concede he can be charming in a very boyish sort of way."

He might have patted her on the head. The arrogance! "You're not going to give up, are you?"

"Give up?" His tone was silky. "Give *you* up?"

"Yes, yes, yes. It's outrageous how you interfere in my life."

"Interference, is that what it's called? Genni, you amaze me."

"Blaine, please." She raised her violet eyes to him. "I'm finding this very painful. Can we stop dancing?"

"Not for a moment. I want to hear something. Did you or did you not tell Hilary you were *very interested* in Colin?"

Her deep sigh expressed despair. "I shall scream if you don't let me go," she said emotionally, so powerfully conscious of him and his body it was simply excruciating.

"No you won't, Genni," he said quietly, but his eyes crackled with light.

"I'm tempted." She threw her head back to stare at him.

"Of course you're tempted. You feel threatened. But you obviously don't want to talk about it."

Wasn't *that* the truth? She was terrified of opening up a Pandora's box. "May I point out Sally is sulking over there."

He sounded amused. "Sally never sulks."

"Oh, for God's sake, I know." She conceded that with a little shake of the head. "But she's obviously missing you." Sally was in fact waving her arms rather wildly, perhaps under the influence of too much champagne. Genni waved back, trying to put a bright reassuring smile on her face. "Is that your orchid she has pinned to her dress?"

"It is." Blaine eased her away from a jitter-bugging couple. "Sally greatly fancies orchids."

"Well you'd know." Her beauty was heightened by a flow of colour to her cheeks. "You go back a long way."

He stared at her. "How fascinating. You sound jealous."

Resolutely she looked away. "Don't be ridiculous. I like Sally. You'd better go and dance with her."

"I'm having a good time as it is dancing with my favourite cousin."

"Not the *whole* damn time."

"*Always,*" he mocked. "In all your moods. How absolutely beautiful you look tonight. Did I tell you?"

Her whole body vibrated. "I certainly don't remember."

"Well I'm telling you now. I so love that dress."

Something in his voice was moving her to tears. "We're too close, aren't we, Blaine," she astounded herself by saying. "Too dangerously close. I'm finally beginning to understand your hold over me." She looked up at him, finding his glance brilliant, searching, mocking? She loved him. Oh, yes! Half hated him, as well. It was difficult to construct her true picture of Blaine. He had played so many roles.

The music stopped, the band struck up again, this time a brighter upbeat tempo.

"I should get back to Colin." She took the opportunity to spring away.

"Why not?" He stood back, a suggestion of sizzling anger about him. "You obviously can't handle being with me."

The ball went on, high spirits gathering momentum as the night wore on. Genni did her very best to try and match the festive mood but by half past one she had to concede defeat. When she left the hall with Lally—it was decided Colin would stay on he was having such a whale of a time—it was to see Blaine and Sally literally tucked away amid the potted palms enjoying what had to be very meaningful conversation. Sally looked unmistakeably a woman in love.

"Do you think Blaine and Sally will ever make a match of it?" Genni asked Lally, not fully aware of her dispirited tone.

"He's not in love with her, dear. You know that. I mean, it's been a kind of no-strings-attached relationship."

Genni gave the older woman a wry sidelong smile. "But she's in love with him, don't forget. She's hung in there.

She's a really nice person. She would make him an excellent wife.''

"In some respects, yes," Lally conceded. "Sally's Outback born and bred. She's a good strong healthy girl with a sensible head on her shoulders. There's joy in her, too. I like that, but she has no *pull*, if you know what I mean. A pull like the moon and the tide. It's a thing apart. I never had it. You do.''

Genni shook her head. "Then I don't really want it. It hasn't worked for me, Lally, even if it were true. I've done something, too, I promised you I wouldn't.''

"Go on. What?" Lally led the way into the homestead, looking faintly aghast.

"I made Blaine angry." Genni gave a brittle laugh. "Yet again. We don't have that simple loving relationship any more.''

"You never did," Lally observed, gripped Genni's hand, looking into the lovely face that was showing strain. "Go to bed, sweetheart," she urged. "I'm praying the two of you will work it all out.''

She fell asleep the minute her head hit the pillow despite her tangle of bittersweet emotions, and the sounds of merrymaking that continued for hours. It would have been understandable had she slept well into the morning but she awoke at first light, wanting to be out of doors. Out in the wild bush where she could think.

A small crowd of guests, who had never gone to bed, was enjoying a lavish buffet breakfast when she went downstairs. No sign of Colin. She waved a hand at those who caught sight of her then quietly slipped away through the back door on her way to the stables. There she saddled up Aurora, a lovely sweet-tempered exhilarating ride.

She made straight across the maze of gullies that lay between the homestead and its small township of satellite buildings and her favourite lagoon the family called The Isis.

It had been named years ago by Blaine's great-grandfather, after the most important of the ancient Egyptian goddesses. Isis, Mother of all things, the lady of all the elements, the beginning of all time.

The name had sprung from the fact this glorious sheet of permanent water, the biggest lagoon on the station, bore the Blue Lotus, the sacred flower of ancient Egypt, in great abundance. It often seemed strange to Genni that this particular waterlily was native to both Australia and North Africa supporting the legends that had existed almost from the time of colonisation of an ancient Egyptian presence in Australia. So many relics had been unearthed in the tropics, artifacts of all kinds, gold coins, gold statues, scarabs, seals, jewellery. Fascinating! In the tomb of Tutakhamon golden boomerangs had been discovered. The boomerang was the Australian aborigine's traditional hunting weapon.

Genni rode on, her troubled feelings, frustration, anger, bewilderment, intense emotionalism eased by the beauty and freshness of the morning. As always the birds accompanied her on her journey, hundreds of little zebra finches, the favourite prey of the falcons and hawks, squadrons of budgerigar in their usual V-shaped formations. White corellas decorated the belt of red-barked trees that ran along the watercourse she took, in stark contrast to the brilliant plumage of the parrots that made their home in the avenues of acacias on the opposite banks. Even at this early hour the mirage was up and about with its extraordinary visual effects, sending a rolling sea of blue waves across the open grasslands where she could see a section of the herd grazing. She adored this desert country.

From an artistic viewpoint, and she hoped to become a good painter one day, there was infinite scope for her brush. The fiery intensity of colours thrilled her; the brilliant dry ochres, the contrasting blazing blue of the cloudless sky, the magnificent sculptural effects of the ancient rocks and monuments, the bleached-white skeletons of desert oaks, and the gnarled and twisted mulgas, the ripple textured, undulating red sand dunes that rolled across the desert like the fabled inland sea.

She loved the vastness of this sun-scorched land the lonely mesas and eroded plateaus, the great network of criss-crossing water channels, billabongs and lagoons that gave life to such a savagely parched area. But even in drought the desert had a majestic beauty. Then to make the spirits soar, after the rains, the miracle of the wildflowers when the entire desert landscape was transformed into a garden on the grandest scale on earth.

She loved Jubilee with a passion that matched Blaine's. The land spoke to her as it did to him. One of the things that had made them so close. Only what she *really* wanted from Blaine couldn't be hoped for. She couldn't even believe in it. There was no person in the world, including her mother, she loved as much as she loved Blaine. Absolutely nobody.

But after that…that…moment out of time, she had to recognise though she had been completely unprepared for it, her feelings had been…sexual. A fantasy. A rapid shift simply because he had looked at her with a different flavour. As a man looks at a woman. This manifestly was what had caused her growing feelings of frustration. The latent powerful urge towards Blaine as a lover.

Was she becoming her mother? Terrible thought. It couldn't be denied both she and Blaine had become increasingly hostile at some level. He standing between her and the things she thought she wanted to do, she straining away from his authority. What was truly frightening was their once beautiful relationship might self-destruct. A thought not to be borne.

Coming down on the emerald lagoon Genni dismounted and led Aurora down the track with its ground cover of delicate little mauve flowers so pretty it was a pity to have to tread on them. Climbing wild passionfruit hung from the trees, the vines covered with a profusion of the pale pink cyclamen-centred flowers. It was wondrously peaceful. So quiet. A large area of the lagoon was floating huge green pads, rising above the leaves the gorgeous hyacinth blue of the lotus lilies. Flowering grasses and reeds fringed the banks, the golden blossoms of a native grevillea flourishing in the rocky terrain of the opposite bank.

Genni walked to the water's edge, bent to splash her heated face in the crystal-clear water, pure enough to drink. A flock of lily trotters were out on the water, some walking delicately on the lily pads, others resting on a raised platform of water grasses. Beautiful images she always carried in her heart.

Last night Colin had as good as asked her to marry him. Perhaps he would have got down on his knees and made a real proposal had she given him a bit more encouragement. But she had held back, no longer sure of anything. She could honestly say she had really enjoyed being with Colin these last months. He was so easy, so undemanding, whereas Blaine for instance was too demanding by far. Blaine was the yardstick for everyone. Add to that he didn't take her seriously. Genni turned away from the water and found a cool spot on the sand, lying back and resting her ash-blond head on her hat. She felt awfully low and it all had to do with you-know-who.

She was half asleep, gently drifting, when Blaine found her. He'd guessed where she was going when someone told him she'd been seen dressed in riding clothes. Genni loved The Isis. It was one of her favourite places on the station.

"Wake up, sleepyhead," he said gently, taking special care not to startle her. He went down on his haunches, brushing her cheek with a flowering frond of grass.

Her beautiful eyes flashed open, staring up into the dark handsome face above her. She wasn't in the least surprised he had found her. Blaine had always read her mind with perfect accuracy. The first rush of joy was replaced by a wariness that showed in her eyes.

"What a night!" Abruptly she sat up only to be further unsettled as he took up a position beside her on the sand.

"They're still partying, would you believe?" He took off his grey akubra and threw it unerringly atop a small nearby rock. "Couldn't you sleep?"

"Couldn't you?"

"Genni, dearest, have you forgotten I don't need much sleep."

"I'm sorry for the way I behaved last night," she said, under the benign influence of the bush.

"I thought you were rejoicing in your fast developing powers."

"I haven't grown up like you wanted, have I?" She spoke softly.

"Why ever would you say that?" His response was instant. Then he spoilt it. "You're still as adorable as ever I remember."

"You're a sarcastic devil, aren't you?" She shook her thick plait back over her shoulder.

"I am if it kills me," he said dryly. "But you're equal to it."

Genni was quiet for a moment trying to straighten things out in her mind. "I love this place," she eventually said.

"I know."

"There's a lot of countrywoman in me."

He gave her his beautiful heartbreaking smile. "I have all the memories, Genevieve."

"Have you? What happened to us, Blaine?"

"In what way?" He looked away across the glittering water.

"We don't communicate like we used to."

"Maybe you're growing up has something to do with it," he suggested.

"Is that what it is?" She spoke quietly. "Colin asked me to marry him last night."

The sensuous mouth twisted. "Do you suppose he'll remember this morning?"

"Can I speak seriously to you at all," she burst out, staring at his handsome profile, the determined jaw.

"Certainly. About *serious* things. If Colin was on the level and not merely half drunk I'd advise against it very strongly."

"Why?" Anger burned in her. "I've got to get married sometime."

"What a ridiculous answer."

"Why do you have to sound as if you're humouring a child?" She reached blindly for a stone and threw it at the water.

"Another example of arrogance," he asked, black-brown brows lifted.

"Well you are. When I seek your opinion you deliberately set out to crush me."

"Oh, Genni." His expression softened unexpectedly. "I can't take this seriously. Colin Garrett is not the man for you. And from where I'm sitting you're not even in love with him."

Awkwardly for such a graceful girl she sprang to her feet, her voice high and defiant. "How would you know?"

"Because I *know* you."

He, too, came to his feet, towering over her like some damned skyscraper, she thought. They faced each other. "What are you trying to prove anyway?" he asked. "That you'd do anything to distance yourself from me and my world?"

She was genuinely shocked. "How can you say that?"

"Maybe it's true." His expression turned dark and broody.

"Can't I have anyone else, Blaine?" she pleaded. "Can't I love anyone else? You treat me as though I'm still a child.

Colin treats me like a woman. That alone is fantastic after you all the time. Now he's asked me to marry him and I'm thinking about marrying him.''

The silver gaze was torched. "If you do anything so *stupid*, so *ill-advised*, I don't think I'd ever want to see you again."

"You can't mean that?" She fell back a little in her dismay.

"I'm a hard man, remember." He held her gaze.

"I know the way your mother abandoned you has never left your mind." She trembled as she said it.

"But I did recover, didn't I, Genni?" He gave a thin smile. "What makes you think I can't recover from you?"

She bit her lip so hard she tasted blood. "Oh, this is so painful, so painful, this taste of bitterness."

"It's a by-product of what's happening between us," he retaliated. "Somewhere in your mind, Genni, you have to discover the truth."

"Maybe the truth is so complicated to bear." She put up her hands swiftly to cup her flushed face.

"There's hardly anything to feel guilty about," he said sharply.

"And what about you?" she challenged him. "You interfere in all my relationships. I never say one word about yours."

"Come on," he jibed, "that's not true." Suddenly amused, but darkly relentless. "Remember Marsha and Sophie?"

"I only remember cracking a few jokes you used to laugh at. Lord, I couldn't even count the number of women in your life. I can't even understand how one of them hasn't grabbed you."

"You're kidding! I wouldn't allow them." He stretched out a hand but she jumped back, pink-cheeked, her breath catching in her throat.

"I'm going to marry Colin." She said it like it was her last defence against him.

"Excuse me, you're *not*. You're not ready for marriage. Especially one that would never work."

"Sez you!" She felt like a woman possessed, unable to control her excitement and anger. "Colin makes me feel like a woman."

"The hell he does!" His voice rasped in her ears, as he looked at her his remarkable eyes full of disgust.

"Anyone can make you feel like a woman," he ground out.

Mutely, knowing what was coming, as vulnerable as a baby, she shook her head, her brain reeling as he did the sheerly unthinkable. He pulled her into his arms with stunning strength, binding her to him, his striking face taut and full of an inner struggle.

She tried to shake herself free of his iron grasp and found it impossible. She had always felt so safe with him, so secure. This would end everything. "Blaine, what are you doing?"

"Just what you think."

And it seemed to her perhaps she always knew what was coming. But how did she endure it? A punishment so exquisite it was a life-changing experience. It was passion. Pure, hopeless, unbridled passion. It raged around them like a great conflagration. She had never in her life felt his mouth moulding hers, opening it, like a man not to be denied, his tongue sliding over her teeth, moving in deep exploration. She had never felt his arms pinning her body. It was ecstasy and violation. He might just reach her soul. The violence of the kiss went on, never losing its blazing energy. It conveyed his old love for her and his present contempt.

When his hand slipped to her breast, claiming it with sovereign mastery, it seemed like a monumental symbolic act. It startled her out of her mind. Enveloped her in such heat her blood felt like lava. She thought she would slip to the ground only he held her so forcefully, intent on demonstrating his physical and sexual supremacy.

He did it brilliantly. She couldn't survive this. She was exposed. One after another Blaine was stripping away all the veils she had worn since she was a child.

She whispered his name with her last breath, conscious his mouth and hands relented at last.

He looked down at her, her lovely pale face, her closed, shadowed eyes, the pulsing rose coloured cushioned mouth. A muscle clenching and unclenching along his strong jaw.

Facing the truth is never easy. Sometimes an unforeseen tragedy could strike. He had thought to liberate Genni from all her confusions but he had only disturbed her further. Worse, terrified her. He had never touched her breasts. Unthinkable. His caressing hand had so shocked her it had filtered through even his mad recklessness. The perfume of her was in his nostrils. It wrapped around him like a cloud.

And now she was stumbling away from him, at first unable to speak, then crying out she hated him, how he oppressed her, near hysterical with shock.

Women how they could destroy a man!

CHAPTER FIVE

The Day After The Wedding That Almost Was

GENNI felt very remorseful when she got off the phone. Remorseful and very sad. What she would really like to do was disappear off the face of the earth. That was Colin. Complaining at the beginning he hadn't been able to speak to her earlier simply because he couldn't get through. That had been Angel. Still nursing the forlorn hope the marriage would go ahead.

Genni had told her no, which led to her mother becoming very angry and calling her "heartless." That from Angel. A classic case of the pot calling the kettle black.

But she had opened up her feelings to Colin. He was kind and in his own way sensitive. A very nice human being who would grow if he could only break away from his dreadful father. She had cried. Colin had cried. In the end both vowing to stay friends forever. It wasn't everyday a jilted bridegroom actually said, "Forget it" when she tried to express her shame, her remorse, her gratitude to him for hearing her out. She had behaved very very badly but Colin convinced her he understood, causing her affection for him, for that was what it *was,* to rise meteorically. Colin had a way with women. Even as she put down the phone, the tears streaming down her cheeks, Genni just knew he wouldn't have the slightest difficulty finding the next. Perhaps that very afternoon.

He hadn't even asked about the engagement ring but of course she would return it. "The monstrosity," Lally had called it. Likewise to be returned the mountain of wedding

95

gifts still on display at Angel's. Instead of using a carrier service perhaps the guests could collect their particular wedding present when they called in on Angel again. Tiffany had told her on the phone with many wicked laughs the "reception" had gone off very well. "You should have been there!" Which was positively weird. Only Tiffany had divined where her heart lay.

Genni dragged herself out of the narrow hospital bed and went into the shower. Darling Em had showed up first thing with a change of clothes for her, so light-hearted one would have thought far from making an exhibition of herself Genni had done something highly commendable. Like marry the Right Man.

She was dressed and waiting when Blaine arrived, putting down the glossy magazine she had been pretending to read. No doubt she would be asked to contribute an article to that very magazine in the near future, citing a nervous breakdown.

"Ready?" So he greeted her, this man who had put her through hell. He was casually dressed in a very sharp red-and-navy open-necked sports shirt with navy jeans, so handsome, so virile, so Blaine, the tears spilled over again. "Come on, Genni. We've got to get through this," he responded with a touch of asperity. No pats on the head. "Dry the tears. Better you feel miserable than having made a hideous mistake."

Wasn't that the truth! "I can't bear to go home. I can not," she appealed to him. "Angel thinks it's still on."

"Angel's ambition has always been to marry you off to the wrong man. I'm not taking you back to your mother, cherub. I'm taking you over to my hotel. To Lally. We fly back to Jubilee this afternoon. I want you to come."

All around her the cymbals clanged. "I suppose you couldn't tell me you *want* me to come," she begged. "You're not simply helping me to hide from the world?"

"Work it out." He picked up her one small case, taking

her arm and leading her out of the room. He seemed in an awful hurry, long legs moving like an athlete in training.

"What about the bill?" she prompted him at reception.

"That's all taken care of. You've told Colin, haven't you?"

"Why do you think I was crying?" she sighed.

"Making big mistakes and learning from them can be character building," he pointed out very dryly.

"Blast you. You're the one who said I had no character to begin with."

They were at the front door when Blaine drew back, staring down at her, brow knitted. "A couple of photographers are outside. I just bet they're waiting for us."

"And I just hope you've got a car." She tried to see around his shoulder. "A *fast* car."

"Your BMW, as it happens."

She looked up at him, her violet eyes huge. "That'll do. We'll walk out nonchalantly."

"Great!" he jeered, his eyes sweeping over her sensational in a simple pink dress. "Put your sunglasses on and don't speak."

It was like running a red light.

Lally had the finest suite in the hotel but when they arrived, Lally, who had spoken to Genni earlier, was nowhere to be found.

"A note here," Blaine read out the few lines jotted down on the hotel notepaper. "Gone off on an errand. Back in an hour."

"Well," said Genni with an enormous effort, sinking into a plush sofa. "Can we talk? *Privately.* I think that's Lally's intention."

"I thought you found talking to me difficult," he countered, making no move towards her.

"I know I upset you." She hung her white-gold head.

Only then he reacted. "Hell, Genni, I've had to take as

much as a man can take. You realize you nearly married Colin.''

''Yes, yes!'' she shuddered. ''I was like out of control.''

''It's time you grew up.''

''I know. I've made a fool of Colin.''

Blaine swivelled towards the balcony that looked out on the magnificent blue harbour. ''The truth is he's none too bright. Or even faithful. Cancelled wedding or not I believe your Colin had a great time last night.''

Genni nearly said, ''Who cares!'' but stopped in time. ''Colin's like that,'' she said tolerantly. ''Anyway, he was very noble.''

Blaine shot her a sparkling admonishing look. ''Oh, shut up.''

''Okay I will. But before I do I want to tell you I love you,'' she cried emotionally. ''I love you in every way possible. I was just hysterical that time you kissed me. The *one* time you kissed me like that. But it blew me away. I kept bumping into things for weeks.''

Blaine walked back and lowered himself into an armchair near her. ''How can a woman be so perverse? You acted like being kissed was life-threatening.''

''It is. It *was*. From you. I must be terribly naive, I wasn't ready for a sexual encounter. We've been family. You've treated me almost like your sister then you throw me in the deep end. In a way it was a kind of terror.'' She extended her hand to him, her heart in her eyes. ''Blaine, I need you. I need you like no one else on earth.''

''As what?'' His brilliant eyes swept her face.

''You want a quick answer?'' Lights seemed to be spilling inside her head.

''I'll never kiss you again if I don't get it.''

''It's crazy,'' she exclaimed, her violet eyes ardent, ''but I want to be your wife. *Your wife.* No one else's.''

''No matter how dangerous?'' Now he moved, lithe as a

panther, sitting down beside her and pulling her across his knees.

She stared up at him. So familiar. The most familiar face in the world. Any yet... "Give me a minute to think."

"No! No! No!" Like a man at the end of his tether, Blaine lowered his head, one hand cupping her delicate skull, holding her tantalizing mouth up to him.

He needn't have bothered. This time Genni was ready. As Blaine dipped his mouth to kiss her she lifted her head to meet him inviting the rapturous crush of desire. Her soul took wings. All the barriers were down. All the deep running, hidden yearnings out in the open.

It was a fever of want that both submitted to, both muttering endearments against the other's tongue. His arms cradled her; one of her arms lay trembling around his neck.

"My Blaine. My Blaine." She murmured his name over and over, her voice shaking with emotion. His broad hand moved to the tilted curve of her breast and she arched her back in desperation overcome by desire. Her skin felt as if it were burning. She had had no idea about love. Now she was beginning to understand... to understand the ecstasy.

"Your heart is in my hands," he whispered passionately, taking the tender weight of her breast.

"I love you. No one else," she whispered back, feeling his mouth brush warmly across her throat before returning to her mouth, his kiss so voluptuous, so dominating...so authoritative...so full of a lifetime's tenderness.

"You're going to marry me. Is that understood?" Briefly he lifted his raven head.

"You want it in writing?" She thought she was dissolving in bliss.

"Not really." His smile held the same old mocking charm. "This time, Violetta, you'll get it right."

Charlotte's Choice
by Barbara Hannay

Dear Reader,

I guess it's no secret that the men of the Australian Outback are gorgeous. From my experience, life in the bush is rugged and dangerous and this environment breeds strong, fit men, who look divine, and are extremely competent and courageous.

It's because these men are such distinct examples of untamed masculinity that I particularly love romances set in the Outback.

I am thrilled to be writing a story in conjunction with Margaret Way, who has created such a wonderful tradition of memorable Outback heroes.

Tall, tough and terrific, Matt Lockhart, my hero in *Charlotte's Choice* is typical of the Outback cattleman. He doesn't waste words, but his feelings run very deep. I think most women would agree these are irresistible qualities. They certainly provided a stumbling block for my English heroine, Charlie.

I hope you enjoy reading this story as much as I loved writing it,

Barbara Hannay

CHAPTER ONE

"CHARLIE, do you know a man called Matt Lockhart?"

Charlie looked up from the postcards she was writing to find her cousin Sarah regarding her with deep suspicion.

"You do know him. You're blushing and looking completely guilty."

"I've heard the name before," Charlie admitted defensively.

"Well, I bet he doesn't know that your *real* name is Lady Charlotte Bellamy. He's on the phone now asking for Charlie Bell."

Charlie jumped to her feet. "What did you tell him?"

"I mumbled something pathetic like—could he hold the line one moment—and then bolted straight here to you."

"I can't speak to him!" Charlie shook her head vehemently. "Sarah, would you be a sweetheart? Please tell him I'm not here and find out what he wants."

"I know what the man wants." Sarah's blue eyes narrowed and she cocked her head to one side as she crossed her arms over her chest. "That's why I thought there must be some mistake." Her voice lowered dramatically. "He wants to talk to you about a *job* you've applied for."

Nodding, Charlie rubbed sweaty palms down her linen skirt. "Yes."

"*Yes?* You mean you *have* applied for a job?"

Charlie nodded again.

"Good grief!" Sarah's mouth opened and closed. Opened once more. "But you're supposed to be here in Australia on a holiday!"

"It's a—a holiday job. I organised a working visa before I left England."

Sarah's eyes rolled heavenwards. "Well, apart from the fact that you appear to be losing your marbles at a very young age, there's a *major* problem," she responded darkly. "This Matt Lockhart fellow thinks you're a man."

"Yes." Charlie sighed. "I thought he might. That's why I can't talk to him, Sarah. He mustn't hear my voice. Would you mind telling him I'll take the job, but, please, don't let him know I'm female. That would spoil everything."

"I'll do no such thing."

Impulsively, Charlie wrung her hands together. "Please, Sarah! I'm begging you! I know it sounds frightfully weird, but I promise it's all above board. Just find out when he wants me to start."

"Start? You mean you really *do* want to work? What kind of job is it? He doesn't sound like someone from your usual circle."

"Hurry! I'll explain later. He'll be ringing long distance from up near the Northern Territory and he'll hang up soon."

"And you want me to let him think you're a fellow?"

Charlie nodded. "Please!" she repeated.

To her intense relief, Sarah began to back out of the room, but she was still shaking her head. "I don't like this, Charlie."

"I'm sorry to ask you to tell a white lie, but trust me, it's fine."

Reluctantly Sarah turned and, straightening her indignant back, left the glassed-in front veranda and returned to the phone in the lounge room.

Charlie let out her breath with a noisy sigh as she ran shaking fingers through her long fair hair. Sarah was a good sort; she wouldn't let her down.

She tried to block out the temptation to eavesdrop on the telephone conversation in the next room by shifting her focus across the street to the bright blue ocean and gleaming sands of Sydney's Bondi Beach. Her cousin's flat provided a wonderful view of amazing bronzed surfers. At any time of day, Charlie could watch them riding their boards down the glassy face of huge waves. She loved the way they made such a dangerous sport look impossibly simple.

Sun and surf. It was easy to understand why Sarah had left England to spend two years living and working in Australia. She was lucky her parents had been so understanding.

Thoughts of parents brought Charlie's gaze back to the postcards she'd been writing. She'd completed the one from Sydney, which she would post this afternoon. And she hoped to find people among Sarah's contacts in the tourist industry, who would be willing to send the other postcards home to Derbyshire at regular intervals. Already, she'd selected a range of popular tourist destinations—the Gold Coast, the Great Barrier Reef and Kakadu National Park.

It was so important to keep her parents reassured she was having a wonderful holiday Down Under. Of course, deceiving them felt bad—very bad. But, under the circumstances, it was a necessary evil. Eventually, her mother and father would be proud of her. Surely.

Sarah's slow footsteps were returning and Charlie looked up, her heart suddenly racing and her hands clenching and unclenching at her sides. "How did it go?" she asked anxiously.

Pausing in the doorway, her cousin took her time as she arranged one slim hip against the door frame. "You're to start next Monday," she said grimly. "Saddle, swag and horse will be provided."

Relief flowed through Charlie, warming her insides like brandy on a midwinter's night. "That's great," she said and sat down suddenly, as her knees threatened to give way.

But Sarah showed no sympathy as she marched slowly, menacingly towards her. "I'm glad *you* think this is great, cousin. But it'll take a lot of convincing before I'm happy."

"I'll explain."

"You bet you will. I haven't a clue what's going on and I don't like being kept in the dark. *And* I don't like being a go-between for you and this Lockhart fellow. *Or* fighting off your parents when they demand to know where you are. You're supposed to be in my tender care." She dragged out a chair and sat down majestically. "Now, tell me in minute detail exactly what hair-brained scheme you've cooked up."

Matt Lockhart grinned as he replaced the receiver. He continued to feel pleased with himself as he sauntered out onto the wide veranda of Sundown Station's homestead, his family's Outback home for the past eighty years.

His head stockman, Arch Grainger, looked up from the paperwork spread all over a small table. "You're smiling. Are we in luck, boss?"

Pulling out a chair, Matt nodded, then sat and stretched his long legs before him. "Problem solved. I've found us another ringer. He's coming next Monday."

"That's a flaming relief!" Arch swatted at a fly with his broad-brimmed akubra hat.

Matt nodded his agreement. Last week, when one of their ringers had broken his leg and needed to be flown to a hospital on the coast, they hadn't liked their chances of finding an emergency replacement.

It was the worst possible time to lose a stockman. With the wet season behind them, the pressure was on for a full-scale muster, but their neighbours were all flat-out with their own musters and couldn't spare anyone.

Arch leaned back in his chair and squinted at Matt. "I assume, by that smug grin you're wearing, that you've got someone who can at least sit on a horse. Most times, when we've pulled in people at the last minute, they've been flipping useless."

Matt shrugged. "His name's Charlie Bell. He has top riding credentials and he reckons he's had plenty of experience on his parents' properties."

"Where?"

Just for a moment, Matt hesitated. "Derbyshire," he mumbled.

"Derbyshire—as in *England?*" Arch didn't try to hide his scorn.

Matt refused to let his stockman rattle him. "Some of the English blokes with rural backgrounds shape up OK after we knock the polish off them in the bush."

Chuckling, Arch shook his head. "He'll lose his polish fast all right. I hope he's a hard worker." He paused. "Does he know how remote this property is?"

"I told him to fly into Camooweal and I'd send someone to meet him."

"You softening him up or something?" Arch asked, scratching stubby fingers through his crinkly grey hair.

Matt scowled. "We don't want this bloke getting lost. But don't worry, once he gets here, I won't be making any excuses for him. I'll make damned sure he understands he has to work as hard as the next man, or he's out on his ear."

Arch nodded and returned to his paperwork, frowning over his rows of figures and Matt stood up and shrugged aside niggling doubts about the faith he was pinning on this Englishman.

Of course everything would be fine.

"You want it all cut off?" Sarah shrieked.

"As short as a boy's," Charlie said firmly. She sat in front of Sarah's dressing table mirror and stared stonily at her reflection.

Behind her, Sarah hovered, shaking her head wildly. "No way!" she shouted. "I can't cut this!" Lifting Charlie's long silken strands, she allowed them to run through her fingers. "It would be a crime against nature to cut this hair off. I simply won't do it. You'll have to go to a salon."

"I can't," Charlie insisted. "I don't want to draw attention to myself and, besides, I don't really have time to organise an appointment in a salon. I've bought good scissors and a dark brown rinse that should cover my own colour."

"Why would you want to turn this long, lustrous, *golden* hair to brown?" exclaimed Sarah.

"You make me sound like a shampoo advertisement."

"You could model for a shampoo advertisement."

"Too bad," snapped Charlie. "I want to look like a boy." And Sarah fell about laughing.

Charlie sighed. Perhaps she *was* asking the impossible of her body.

"Look at you!" Sarah gasped when she eventually gathered her mirth under control. "You're an English Rose! You have a peaches-and-cream complexion, delicate features, big green eyes with lashes so long I'm sure they're illegal and all this lovely hair!"

"And I also have hair dye, scissors, and tanning lotion." Charlie held out her hands in front of her. She inspected her long, manicured fingernails and pulled a face. "I'll have to cut my nails really short, as well."

Sarah frowned, hands on hips. " Even if we did deal with the hair, the skin and the nails, there's no way you can disguise your chest."

Charlie looked down at her offending breasts. "Aren't there ways of flattening them or something?"

"My dear Charlie," Sarah sighed, leaning back against the dressing table and looking down at her cousin with the air of an exasperated elder. "Do you have any idea what life is like on an Outback mustering camp?"

"No," Charlie admitted. "That's why I'm going there. I want a taste of something completely different. I want a heightened perspective on life. I want—" She paused. This burning desire for an adventure as different as possible from her staid and safe life in England was much more than a simple want. "I *need* to get into the Outback. I have to face danger and hardship."

"Oh, you'll get that all right," Sarah reassured her. "And

heat, dust, flies—not to mention thousands of noisy, nasty, smelly cattle. And the men!''

"They're noisy, nasty and smelly, too?"

"Some of them. You'll find living in the Outback is like visiting another planet! Believe me, you'll have enough to deal with without trying to pretend you're a man at the same time.''

"But they might send me packing as soon as they see I'm a woman," Charlie wailed.

"They might," Sarah agreed. "But then again, Matt Lockhart sounded pretty desperate on the phone. And there are plenty of women who work in the Outback—Australian women that is.''

"If you won't cut my hair then at least help me dye it brown and get this tanning stuff on," Charlie pleaded. "Then I might look more like an Australian girl.''

Sarah's eyebrows rose sceptically and she let out a sigh. "I can't believe I'm doing this." She picked up the box of hair colour and began to read the instructions.

Charlie's hand closed over hers and squeezed gently. "Thanks so much, Sarah. You've no idea how much this means to me.''

"I must say I'm puzzled and curious," Sarah admitted as her blue gaze met Charlie's green. "How on earth did a girl with your background get obsessed with a crazy idea like this?''

Charlie looked back at her cousin with a bemused smile. She'd often asked herself where this desire for an Outback adventure had started. The yearning to escape from her restricted lifestyle had been with her ever since she was young. Had it begun with the book in her grandfather's library? A huge, heavy book with full-page, glowing pictures of a vast, red and mysterious, sun-drenched landscape, enormous mobs of cattle and tanned, fit men on beautiful horses. Those pictures had completely captivated her.

And then there had been her Uncle Albert's stories of

adventure when he came home after sailing around the world in a little boat single-handed. From then on she'd craved for an adventure of her own.

"I've always loved the idea of adventure and challenge," she told Sarah. "If I'd been the boy Daddy wanted so badly, he would have been happy to let me prove myself as a man and have an Outback adventure."

"I would have thought fighting your way up to a top job in London's art world would have been challenge and adventure enough."

"I did that because it was what Daddy wanted me to do," Charlie explained as she bent forward over the sink to wet her hair.

"And you're jolly good at it. Brilliant from what I hear."

"I also have to find someone to marry—to help the family out—someone titled preferably. I'm supposed to be catching someone disgustingly rich and well bred."

"Marrying into a title and money. How awful for you," Sarah scoffed as she pulled on rubber gloves and squeezed hair dye into a bowl.

"You should count your lucky stars your father is the *second* son of an earl. The pressure on poor Daddy and Mother and on me for that matter, to keep up the family estate is sending him to bankruptcy and an early grave."

"I've heard the old place is virtually crumbling around your ears. Hold still," Sarah added as she applied the dye to Charlie's damp hair. "And I suppose you're expected to save the day."

"Yes," sighed Charlie. "And we all know how thin on the ground gorgeous titled men with pots of money are. There are one or two but most of them are PCBs."

"Pardon?"

"Pale, chinless and boring."

"Poor Charlie," murmured Sarah sympathetically. "I must say I do value my freedom. But then again," she added, giving her cousin a reassuring pat on the head through the rubber glove, "if anyone can snare one of the gorgeous variety, I'm sure you can."

"Nevertheless, I need one adventure before I have to go back and be the dutiful daughter. But I knew if I told Mother what I was really planning, she'd have another attack. Her blood pressure—"

"Aunt Vera's blood pressure is conveniently unreliable," muttered Sarah.

"I want them to relax and think I'm having a nice holiday. Eventually, I'll tell them what I've really been doing."

Sarah piled Charlie's darkened hair high on her head. "OK. I suppose we can keep them happy."

"And I'm going to have my once in a lifetime chance for real excitement," Charlie affirmed, ignoring the little ripples of doubt and panic as she thought about what might lie ahead. She screwed up her face. "Ouch! That dye is getting in my eye."

CHAPTER TWO

MATT leapt from his vehicle before the dust had time to settle, slammed the door shut and marched fiercely towards the ringers' cottage. Angry as a maddened bull, he kicked open the rusty metal gate. "Where is he?" he bellowed.

In two strides he cleared the steps then paused at the open front door and peered down the dark central hallway of the cottage. Bedrooms lined either side. A young ringer stuck his head out of the first doorway. "Who're you looking for, boss?"

"The new fellow, Bell," Matt barked. "Charlie Bell."

The ringer's eyes popped and his Adam's apple slid up and down in his skinny neck as he cocked his head to indicate down the hallway. "End room on the left."

"Got it!" muttered Matt and, with a curt nod, continued his march down the hall, hands bunched into fists and swinging at his sides. He'd just wasted the best part of a day driving the dusty four-hour round trip into Camooweal while this new chum, Charlie Bell, had taken it into his head not to wait for him, but to hitch a ride out to Sundown on the mail truck. He was furious!

The flaming hide of the fellow! He'd been told to wait at the airstrip.

Reaching the end room, Matt didn't stop to knock, but roughly shoved the door open.

Then he stopped.

All he could see was a backside—a very neat backside. A very *feminine* rear end inside skintight, pale cream, very expensive jodhpurs. As backsides went, it rated as the most womanly and desirable he'd ever seen.

It disappeared as its owner stopped rummaging in her

112

backpack and whirled around to face him. Big, startled green
eyes and a soft pink mouth rounded in surprise.

Matt's own mouth hung wide, *wide* open. For long seconds he stood gaping at this female. As well as the expen-
sively cut jodhpurs, she wore gleaming hand-tooled leather
riding boots and a simple white blouse that couldn't hide
her other womanly parts. Her hair was braided into a silky
brown plait that had flopped over one shoulder.

She was beautiful.

Damn it to hell!

Matt shook his head.

And shut his mouth.

Opened it again. "What the hell are you doing here?" he
managed to ask at last.

Her pretty pink lips tilted ever so slightly into a nervous
smile. "I'm Charlie Bell."

"The devil you are."

She held out a slim hand. "You must be Mr. Lockhart."

Her hand felt cool and super-soft as Matt shook it. He
dropped it quickly and shoved his own calloused palms deep
into the pockets of his jeans. And he glared at her as he tried
to come to terms with this latest disaster. "Why didn't anybody tell me you were a woman?"

Her gaze dropped to the floor and he watched her cheeks
grow an amazing shade of pink. But when she looked back
at him again, her eyes held his steadily. "I thought there
was a very good chance you wouldn't have been interested
in me if you knew I was female. Especially as I'm an
English woman."

"You're dead right," Matt snapped back at her. He was
getting over the shock and his anger was flooding back. He
turned and kicked the metal leg of her bed. "Hell! What a
mess!"

"I hope not, Mr Lockhart. If you'll give me a chance to
prove my worth, I'm sure you won't regret taking me on."

Her voice was cool and calm, very polite and plummy

English, reminding Matt of some of the BBC television programs his mother used to watch. *Polite?* Who was she trying to kid? He swung back to her. "It was jolly rude the way you jumped on the mail truck instead of waiting for me."

"Again I must apologise," she said softly. Pearly white teeth toyed briefly with her pouty lower lip. "I was afraid that if we met at the Camooweal airport as you suggested, you would put me straight back on the plane."

"Darn right I would." Matt thrust an angry jaw forward. "Listen, Miss Bell." He glanced quickly at her left hand. "I presume it's *Miss?*"

"I'm not married if that's what you're asking."

"You seem to be very sneaky about protecting your interests. I don't like that. This might be some little party trick you've dreamed up to tell over dinner when you get home—"

"No!" Charlie interrupted. She stared at him appalled. How could she make Matt Lockhart understand? "This is very important to me."

"And it's damn serious for me! You were told to wait. That was the agreement." His dark eyes speared her with deadly, no-nonsense intent. "Now listen. I'm used to having instructions carried out to the letter. If I tell someone to wait somewhere for me, he waits. Out here, you just do what you're told. If you can't follow instructions, people's lives can be at risk."

"Yes, Mr. Lockhart."

"I don't want a tourist. I need a skilled man. Someone who knows the job and who's prepared to work hard. Being a ringer is no picnic. It's rough, hard, and hot."

"I was hoping it would be."

Matt blinked. His dark brows drew together in a puzzled frown as his eyes studied her. "You were hoping it would be...?" For a shade too long, his eyes travelled over her. "Are we both talking about mustering work?"

Charlie gulped. Sudden awareness of the molten, brown

heat of Matt Lockhart's unflinching gaze and the leashed in power of his hard, work-toughened body flustered her. Rough, hard and hot? *What in heaven's name was she thinking?*

What did he think she was thinking?

She wiped a trickle of sweat from her face with the back of her hand. "I—I know work in the Outback is tough. It's what I want."

"Why?" Matt challenged.

For months she'd had so many answers at her fingertips, but for the moment, they deserted her.

"Is your life lacking excitement?"

Charlie took a deep breath, hoping it would help to hold back the blushes his question triggered. Her life's lack of excitement was exactly why she was here, but Matt Lockhart posed his question so scornfully that she had no intention of admitting to any such failings.

His gaze switched to her pack, open on the floor, revealing an assortment of clothing—mainly underwear. With her foot, Charlie tried to flip the canvas flap of the bag over the exposed items. Best not to provide Matt Lockhart with too many images of her femininity.

Straightening her shoulders, she returned his steady gaze. "My life is exactly how I want it, thank you very much, Mr. Lockhart. I understand your anger, but is there something you feel I don't understand?"

"Of course there is!" For a moment, he sighed impatiently and lowered his head. Raising a hand, he kneaded the back of his neck. Then, without warning, his gaze flicked back to her. He straightened and his hand fell to his side. "We don't play games out here. We've got to rely on each other, so we need to be able to trust everyone. A con artist is quickly caught out."

She frowned. "A con artist?"

"Yes." The faintest suggestion of a smile twitched his lips. "A fraud, a trickster."

Charlie stifled a gasp of dismay. If Matt Lockhart knew her real identity, would he consider her a fraud?

Her stomach tightened, but she wouldn't let this man intimidate her. She was sure she could do the work if only she had half a chance. And she certainly hadn't been brought up as Lady Charlotte, daughter of an Earl, to be put down by an obnoxious young Australian cattleman.

Drawing in a steadying breath, she held his gaze. "Mr. Lockhart, I'm not going to beg you for this position. But I understand that you need to employ someone and that your chances of getting another stockman on short notice, at this time of the year, are limited. I happen to be available and I believe I am suited to the job."

The silence that greeted her speech stretched to an uncomfortable length, but eventually Matt's face finally softened into an amused grimace.

"You put together a persuasive case," he drawled.

She'd been holding her breath and now she released it in a heartfelt sigh of relief.

Too soon. He was frowning again. "You can stay on a galloping horse?"

"I certainly can." She'd been riding since she was five years old.

"Let me see your hands."

Oh, dear. Nervous once more, Charlie held out her small, delicate hands. Thank goodness she'd cut her nails very short. Matt touched them tentatively with his fingertips and turned them over, palms up. She hadn't applied the tanning lotion to her hands for fear it would look too artificial, so they were still milky white and her wrists were ridiculously slim, with fine blue veins making them look even more fragile.

As Matt stared, she realised that they smelt of the flowery hand cream she'd used, night and morning, every day since she was fifteen. Now she regretted the habit.

He was frowning and looking rather put out, almost as if

he'd read her future in her palms and hadn't liked what he discovered. "You won't be much use throwing bullocks," he said after some time.

"You need me to throw bullocks?" It was impossible to keep the squeak of panic out of her voice.

"I might. And how are you at castrating calves?"

"Castrating?" she parroted dully, her stomach churning at the very thought.

The faint creases 'round his eyes deepened. "I'm afraid we can't let every baby bull grow up to be a daddy."

"No. Of course not," Charlie blustered. She realised Matt was still holding her hands and he was smiling.

The realisation must have struck him at the same moment. He dropped her hands and stepped back. The smile vanished.

"There was no mention of tasks like that when I applied," she argued.

"Most blokes know what's expected of a ringer."

Charlie's hopes plummeted. It would be terrible to be turned away now, after the long flight north and the hot and dusty drive across from Camooweal. She'd made it this far and she didn't want to go back. She'd never seen country like it—wide, flat, sundried plains cut, every so often, by the most beautiful deep blue waterways, fringed by red rocks, huge trees and teeming with bird life.

"I've hired women to work as jillaroos on this property before," Matt admitted slowly. "They've all been good workers. Of course they weren't poms—er—I mean English and they knew what they were in for." He propped his hands on his hips. "But as you've so kindly pointed out, on this occasion I haven't really got much choice."

"That's right."

"But what's the real reason you've come here?"

Oh, boy! She needed to take this carefully. Charlie wet her lips. "I've dreamed about this since I was a little girl."

"Really?"

"Don't you have dreams, Mr. Lockhart?"

He looked startled by her question. There was an awkward silence. "We're leaving for the first mustering camp in the morning. I guess you'd better come with us." His eyes narrowed. "But if you don't shape up, we can't afford to have you slowing us down. You'll be sitting around all by yourself waiting for that mail truck to take you out again."

Turning abruptly, he disappeared through her door.

"Thank you," Charlie called to his retreating back, although she was feeling so rocked by the encounter, she could hardly remember what she was thanking him for.

In thirty seconds, he was back in her doorway, his big brown hand gripping the lintel. "Just thought I'd better warn you. Don't bother bringing any of those fancy, pale-coloured jodhpurs." His eyes rested on her lower regions for a shade longer than was polite. "This isn't a gymkhana and they'll only get ruined."

"Thanks," she said again, feeling strangely better.

It was pitch black when she heard the loud banging and a dog barking. Struggling to surface from a particularly pleasant dream, Charlie rolled over and then settled more comfortably, hugging her pillow closer. Now what had she been dreaming? A strong, tanned hand was holding hers...leading her somewhere enticing...and she was tingling with delicious expectation...amazing excitement...

More noises roused her, and the moment that trembled on the edge of bliss was swept roughly aside. Now she realised she was hearing bedsprings creaking, boots echoing on wooden floorboards, doors opening and shutting...

Good grief! She shot up in bed and groped for her watch, couldn't read the time in the dark, but the sounds were enough to alarm her. The ringers were up! It was morning! As if to prove her right, there was a sharp rat-a-tat on her door and a strong Australian accent called through the dark, "Ready, Charlie? Breakfast's on."

In one movement, her feet hit the floor as she dragged off

her nightshirt. *"Hurry!"* she urged her fumbling fingers and she pulled on a bra, shirt and jeans. Throughout the cottage there was silence. Had all the others left already? She was the last one? Stumbling across the room, she tried to drag on her high-sided riding boots as she ran. Impossible! There was nothing for it but to sit in the middle of the floor and pull them on carefully.

Done! She dashed down the hallway, roughly braiding her hair with frantic fingers. Across the stretch of dying grass to the homestead kitchen. From inside, she could see the yellow spill of light and hear the low hum of men's voices. Oh, no, she hoped she wasn't noticeably late. She stepped through the kitchen doorway.

Sudden silence. Ten pairs of masculine eyes swung in her direction. Her heart pumped fretfully as she tucked her shirt into the waist of her jeans. "Good morning."

"Morning, mate."

"Morning."

There was a muttered chorus of greetings and the men quickly returned to the serious business of devouring sausages, bacon and tomatoes. As she quietly approached the stove and piled her plate with fried tomatoes and toast, only one pair of eyes from the far end of the long pine table continued to watch her. Dark, wary eyes in a tanned, ruggedly handsome face—the face of her boss.

The sight of him caused Charlie's own eyes to widen. Last night, she'd noticed Matt Lockhart was good-looking, but she was too busy fighting for her right to stay on his property to dwell on the matter.

But now, as he sat with a group of other men, his looks stood out in the way a masterpiece claims attention in an art gallery. Beneath his dark, rough and tumbling hair, his face presented a pleasing balance between the strong lines of his cheekbones, nose and jaw and the sensitivity in his dark eyes and enticing mouth. The deep blue, open-necked, cotton shirt did little to conceal the breadth of his shoulders. He had a natural beauty that was intensely masculine.

Realising she was staring, Charlie quickly dropped her gaze and took a spare seat between two ringers and began to eat. She glanced at her watch. Five fifteen.

Her first day in the bush had begun.

"Hey, Dinga!" someone called.

She looked around curiously.

A scrawny fellow with a missing tooth grinned at her. "That's you, isn't it? Charlie Bell? Dinga-ling Bell?"

"I guess it must be."

"How long have you been in Australia, Dinga?" he asked.

"Two weeks."

Her answer was greeted by a knowing smirk followed by a chuckle.

"I'm sorry," Charlie said as she smiled back politely, "I didn't catch your name."

"Crocodile Dundee," the fellow replied with another self-satisfied grin.

The young ringer opposite snorted with nervous laughter, but the man beside her said quietly, "Don't take any notice of him, Charlie. He's Ted Smith and he thinks he's a comedian."

Charlie resumed eating. But all around her the men seemed to be finishing their meal, swilling down coffee and scrambling to their feet. Her appetite had only just begun to swing into gear and now she looked sadly at her untouched coffee and half-eaten tomatoes.

"You need a bit longer?" Matt called to her as he strode past, looking businesslike.

"No, no, I'm ready," she answered smartly, jumping to attention and joining the line of men as they filed out into the pale dawn outside.

Matt spoke to her again. "You've put your swag and gear in the back of the truck?"

Charlie looked at the truck, parked just beyond the ringers' quarters. Its tray back was piled with canvas swags, packs, saddles and horse blankets. "Um—no. My stuff's still in my room. Shall I run and get it?"

"Might be an idea." His growl was edged with sarcasm. "We need to get going."

Cursing herself for not asking enough questions the previous evening, Charlie dashed into her room and snatched up her pack. She shoved her hairbrush and nightshirt into it and wrenched the zipper shut. Hoisting it onto one shoulder, she crammed her wide-brimmed hat on her head, grabbed the swag she'd been given the night before and gripped it tightly between her arm and her body. It was surprisingly heavy. Finally, in her other arm, she took up the saddle the head stockman had given her and, staggering under the weight and bulk of her load, struggled back to the truck.

Feeling like an ungainly, overloaded camel, she refused to make eye contact with any of the men as she wobbled towards the truck. A metal stirrup banged painfully against her shin as she went.

Matt fell in beside her. "Here, let me take something," he offered.

"I'm fine," she answered stiffly, keeping her chin high and her eyes focused on her destination—the waiting back of the truck. Of course, she didn't see the pothole right in the middle of the road. Stepping into it was enough to upset her precarious balance and send her toppling sideways.

Fair and square on top of Matt Lockhart.

The pack, swag, saddle and Charlie—an avalanche of leather, canvas and woman bowled Matt flat on his back. For seconds, he lay stunned as he came to terms with his horizontal position. A thick braid of soft hair filled his mouth and a struggling, gasping body pinned him to the ground. Sharp gravel dug through his shirt and into his back.

"If I can just get rid of this pack I'd be able to move," he heard Charlie mutter close to his ear. She grunted, wriggled and squirmed in an effort to untangle herself. It was an unfortunate series of movements. Matt couldn't help his reaction. With her sweet smell filling his nostrils and her soft, womanly curves pressing and thrusting wildly against him, his body literally sprang to attention.

He held his breath, hoping she wouldn't notice. Hoping the circle of grinning witnesses wouldn't guess.

But Charlie noticed all right. Her desperate movements came to a sudden halt and her green eyes, inches from his, stared down at him, their expression at first stunned and then alarmed. Her cheeks grew an even deeper shade of that amazing pink he'd witnessed yesterday.

This was beyond ridiculous. Matt gripped her by both shoulders and levered her and her gear up and away from him, but he was acutely aware as he did so, of her warmth deserting him. Jerking his head sideways in the direction of a row of dusty riding boots, he barked, "Somebody help her!"

At last there was action. The boots moved forward. Items were lifted. Charlie was helped to her feet. Rolling sideways, he grabbed his hat from the ground and jumped upright. "Let's get moving. We've wasted enough time," he growled, not wanting to think about the strange sense of loss he felt as he pushed Charlie away from him.

Without looking at anyone else, he swung his long legs up into the driver's seat and started the engine. Ahead of him, Arch started up the horse truck and the cook moved off with the ute. Ringers climbed into whatever space was available in the backs of the vehicles. It was only as he accelerated and rolled the truck forward, that Matt wondered if perhaps he should have offered Charlie the spare passenger's seat next to him.

Forty minutes later the convoy halted.

By then, Charlie had been through a painful cavalcade of emotions from embarrassment, through anger to frustration.

She couldn't have begun her stint at Sundown on a worse footing.

She had done her level best to squash memories of Matt Lockhart lying beneath her and she certainly didn't want to think about the sudden quickening of her response when she found herself pinned against his hard, muscle-packed length.

Her body had played cruel tricks on her. The thrust of Matt's arousal had sent an explosion of heat coiling through her and there'd been a flaring, totally inappropriate desire to taste the sun-drenched skin suddenly so close to her lips.

These reactions had shocked her. She'd come out here for adventure, not to harbour lurid thoughts about her new boss.

During the journey, Charlie refocused her attention on the surrounding landscape. Wide and red-brown, it was exactly like the photos in her grandfather's book. And she was relieved when they reached their destination—a small corrugated iron shed in what seemed like the middle of nowhere. Now there would be plenty of work and she could centre all her concentration on her job.

The men set about unloading horses and motorbikes and Matt led a strong black gelding and a slim but strong-looking chestnut mare towards Charlie. Cautiously, she forced her eyes up to meet his. But if he was annoyed by the early morning mishap, she could see no sign in his face or his manner.

"This is Duchess." He held the mare's reins out to her and spoke in a let's-get-down-to-business tone of voice. "You'll find she has a smooth stride and she loves her work. As soon as she sees cattle, her head goes up and she's prancing, ready for action."

"Hello, Duchess." Charlie rubbed the mare's silky hide. "She's beautiful," she told Matt with a smile.

From beneath his battered akubra, he squinted towards the distant pale shimmer on the horizon. "Two helicopters have been working the mobs in towards this direction," he explained. "We'll go out and pick them up near bore 55 and then we should be able to move them to bore 67 by lunch-time.''

Charlie nodded. The numbers of the bores meant little to her and her empty stomach rumbled at the thought of the long, hot, hungry hours till lunchtime. Still, here she was, about to have her first real taste of adventure. Surely food was irrelevant!

Matt mounted his horse, and sitting tall and straight in the saddle, began to head off. Over his shoulder, he called. ''When you're ready, you'd better come with me.''

Charlie wasn't sure this was a good idea. Now, if she made any mistakes, her boss would be the first to notice. It made no sense at all that a little fillip of pleasure danced in her chest at the thought of spending a whole morning at his side.

Moving some distance away, Matt waited and watched as Charlie saddled up Duchess. He watched her talking softly to the mare as she worked and he noted the ease with which she adjusted the bridle and girth straps before neatly slipping her boot into the stirrup and swinging a long, graceful leg high over Duchess's back. She settled into the Australian stock saddle as smoothly as a wood duck landing on the surface of a dam and when she took up the reins, it required only the slightest nudge of her knees to edge Duchess for-ward.

The hard knot of tension between his shoulder blades be-gan to ease. At least Charlie Bell looked at home on the back of a horse.

Turning his mount's head to the west, he gave a nod to the men and took off. Soon the sound of hooves drumming the hard earth surrounded him. Out of the corner of his eye he could see Duchess's nose. Charlie was still keeping up.

Within fifteen minutes, they found the herd. Charlie, hot and sweaty, but exhilarated by the ride, pushed her hat back and stared. She'd never seen so many cattle in one group.

They stretched in a patchwork quilt of grey and brown clear to the horizon.

Matt yelled instructions and the men broke away, riding off in groups of two or three. Finally he called to Charlie. "You come with me and we'll check out the creek. There'll be stragglers down there we need to get out."

Running her tongue over dusty lips, she nodded. Her first task. Nervously, she followed Matt towards the dry creek bed. Sure enough, a string of cattle had wandered down there, no doubt hoping to find water. To her relief, Duchess seemed to know exactly what to do. When she paced up and down beside the beasts, they turned and began to plod slowly back up the bank. One leading animal trotted towards the main mob and many of the others followed.

Duchess was brilliant. If a straggler tried to move away, she could turn in an instant and head it back in the right direction. On several occasions, when the directions changed often and fast, Charlie needed all her riding skill to stay with her mount.

Eventually, they cleared the creek of straggling cattle and joined the men who were moving the rest of the herd back east. Charlie was aware of Matt's quiet vigilance but he seemed happy enough with her effort. She felt a glow of relief mingled with a sense of accomplishment.

Their aim was to reach the holding yards by midafternoon. Overhead, the sun burned high and scorching hot. Charlie was grateful for her wide-brimmed hat and she rolled her long sleeves down to cover her arms. The cattle rumbled along in a bewildering press of bodies, the calves and cows calling to each other through the swirling dust. Somewhere behind her, a stockwhip cracked.

She allowed herself a little grin of triumph. *I'm doing this! I'm actually mustering cattle in Outback Australia!*

A picture of the art gallery in London where she normally worked flashed into her mind—an elegant, ancient building of grey stone, its third floor filled with offices where thin, serious-faced men sat behind enormous leather-topped desks and murmured into phones in hushed, well-bred voices. Women, dressed in expensive power suits, would be running around looking busy or bored, depending on who they wanted to impress.

She smiled. Now, at the bottom of the globe, swaying in a saddle under a blazing sun and surrounded by suffocating dust, her usual life seemed unreal, like something she'd read about in a magazine.

A sudden brisk wind flashed across the plains, bringing her straight out of daydreams and into the present. It wasn't a fresh, cooling breeze, but a hot blast of gritty sand that stung her cheeks and flew into her mouth. Just a little ahead of her, the wind picked up a ringer's hat and sent it skimming along the ground. He dismounted to retrieve it. At that instant, his horse bolted.

Duchess and Charlie reacted together. Her knees pressed the mare's flanks and Duchess leapt forward. Within seconds, they were galloping after the escaping horse. Charlie was sure it was more good luck than anything, but as she drew alongside the runaway, she managed to lean over and catch its bridle.

Feeling mightily pleased with herself, she trotted back to the ringer. It was the breakfast comedian, Ted Smith, and he was standing hat in hand, looking just a touch shame-faced. "Good on ya, Dinga," he said with a grumpy grin. "Thanks."

Matt came up to join them. "Good save," he called to Charlie.

She stifled a ripple of pleasure and replied, "You should thank Duchess. She did all the work."

Matt angled her a quick smile and nodded as he moved ahead of them once more.

After he swung himself back into the saddle, Ted Smith leaned forward. "You know, Dinga, you're right about Duchess being clever. She's the boss's favourite mare, the best of the lot. He usually rides her. Must be because you're a shelia that he gave her up for you.''

He flicked his reins and dashed away before Charlie could reply. But if he'd hoped to take her down a peg or two, making her confused and guilty instead of proud about her morning's work, he'd achieved his purpose.

She was still feeling subdued, as well as dreadfully hot and very hungry, when they reached bore 67 close to midday and stopped for lunch. The horses were secured and sandwiches of corned beef and pickles were extracted from the tucker box and handed around. Ravenous, Charlie ate her share as quickly as the men.

"No point in trying to push the cattle in the hottest part of the day. They get testy, so we usually take a bit of a spell," Matt told her. He handed her a big chipped enamel mug of tea before wandering back to join a group of men resting some distance away in the shade of a straggly stand of gum trees.

Feeling like an outcast, Charlie considered her options as she sipped her tea. She could try to edge her way into the men's cosy little circle, or she could sit by herself when she found some more shade…or she could try to cool off.

She decided to head for the nearest water. They'd come past it on their way in—a big pond built up above the ground level. One of the men had explained that they called it a turkey nest dam. It was far enough away from the others for privacy. It looked relatively clean—and very cool. Exceedingly wet—the perfect antidote for her hot and dusty state.

When she reached the dam, Charlie looked cautiously behind her. The men were a long way off and either dozing, with hats over their faces, or smoking and chatting quietly—absorbed in their own stories. She made her way down the rammed earth bank to the edge of the water. Now it was impossible for the men to see her, but just to be sure, she crouched behind a bush while she quickly stripped before lowering herself in.

Bliss.

She'd never felt so instantly refreshed. The cool water swirled around her, washing away the dust and cooling her skin, rejuvenating her flagging energy levels. Striking out boldly, she swam towards the middle of the dam, taking pleasure in the freedom of her body unencumbered by clothing. She tumbled playfully in the deeper water before switching to a leisurely breaststroke.

Drifting slowly back towards the bank, Charlie rolled onto her back and floated. Completely relaxed, she let her limbs hang loose and her head drop back. Water lapped at her breasts and between her thighs and she was free as an aimless cloud drifting in a soft, blue heaven. What a wonderful idea this was.

If Mother could see me now, she thought with a giddy giggle.

"Listen to me and do exactly what I tell you."

The cold menacing voice sounded close.

Fear sliced into her. Terrified, she whirled and thrashed the water as she turned to see who had crept up behind her!

"Oh-my-God!"

CHAPTER THREE

MATT stood on the bank, feet planted wide apart, holding a rifle and looking ready to use it.

Charlie splashed wildly in the water as she tried to cover herself.

He took another menacing step forward and she heard a hair-raising *click-click* as he worked the bolt of the rifle.

Trying to crouch low beneath the dam's surface, her terror increased. She knew that sound. It meant he'd just loaded his weapon!

"Don't splash. Don't make a sound and just get out of the water," he said, his voice cold and hard.

This was insane! The fierce look in his eyes shocked her. How had this happened? She was alone, in one of the remotest corners of the earth, with a handful of strange men and a wild-eyed boss with a gun. Worse still, he was demanding that she get out of the water. *Stark naked.*

"Go away, or I'll start screaming for help!" she yelled at him.

"You little fool! What do you think I'm trying to do? You've got to get out of the water. It's not safe in there."

Not safe in the dam? She'd never considered that. But from Charlie's perspective, nowhere looked safe anymore. There was certainly no way she would parade naked in front of him. "Turn your back," she demanded.

He shot her an exasperated grimace. "I can't. I don't dare and if I do have to fire, just swim like hell for the bank."

Something in his tone—a less threatening and yet more urgent note, a change from anger to desperate insistence—alerted Charlie that perhaps he wasn't planning murder and

129

that something was wrong. Very wrong. She realised then that she had no choice. She had to do as he said.

With trembling limbs, she began to swim towards the bank. Matt watched her every move.

When she reached the edge, fear of staying in the water warred with fear of getting out. She tried to crouch in the shallows. "What is it?" she cried as she steeled herself to leave the water. "Are there snakes in here?"

"No," he said slowly. "A big lizard."

At that, she dashed past him to frantically grab at her clothes on the bank. Clutching her jeans and shirt in front of her, she discovered to her surprise that Matt was paying no attention to her state of undress. His rifle was raised to his shoulder and he was staring intently at a little circle of bubbles in the middle of the dam. "Just back up slowly to the top of the high bank," he said quietly.

She fled.

With a rush of relief, Matt lowered his rifle, but kept his eyes trained on the water. He gave Charlie enough time to get dressed before he walked up the bank to join her. When he reached the top, he was aware of her silence as he pulled back the bolt of the rifle and caught the brass cartridge when it ejected. He slipped it into his pocket.

She did up the last of the buttons on her shirt and he was aware of the way the thin cotton clung to her wet skin and how her long plait left an intriguing wet trail down her back. He'd already seen enough to know this woman was a walking, talking centrefold model. So now he did his darned best to avoid looking at anything below her neck. Relieved that at last the danger was over, he sent her what he hoped was an encouraging grin.

She scowled back.

"For a moment there I thought you were going to argue with me," he told her.

Angry sparks flared in her glass-green eyes and she snapped back at him like a bad-tempered pup. "What's this all about? Some Outback Aussie joke you like to play on English girls?''

He should have bawled her out—given her an earful about how stupid she'd been—even threatened to sack her on the spot—but instead, when she glared at him in that sassy way, Matt found he was grinning. ''You were getting a bit too close to our wildlife,'' he explained.

''There's a—a crocodile?''

''That's right. He's about sixteen feet long and he's been taking my cattle. Who knows how many creatures he's death-rolled in the bottom of this dam.''

Charlie's composure disintegrated in an instant. It was as if someone had let off a grenade inside her and she was collapsing piece by piece. The colour fled from her face and she began to shake violently.

Sure that her legs were giving way, Matt reached out to support her. ''Take it easy.''

''I'm OK,'' she cried, flinching away from him. ''You can keep your distance.''

Frowning, he stepped back again, his big hands falling loosely to his sides.

Her chin lifted defensively. ''I thought crocodiles were only in big streams and waterholes.''

''The river's only a couple of kilometres away. He must have got up in here during the big wet. This whole area was flooded.''

''Oh, God!'' she whispered, the last shreds of her bravado gone. She turned a pale face to him and fixed him with big, frightened eyes, outlined by charcoal lashes.

Something as big and hard as a boulder wedged in Matt's throat.

''What else can I do wrong out here?'' she cried, her lower lip trembling and making him think of a full-blown rose, soft and pink and about to fall apart.

And he suddenly found himself thinking that if they'd met somewhere else—at a party, with music and champagne and dancing, not out here on a muster in the back of beyond—who knows what might have happened?

In a pig's eye! Where had that idiot idea come from? He was going soft in the head. Nevertheless, he heard himself tell her, "I should have warned you not to go swimming. Don't worry. You're doing OK. You're doing well."

Her lips remained in an unsmiling tight line as she sat down to haul on her boots. "But you'd better hurry," he added gruffly. "We've got to get this mob moving again." And he quickly decided it was a good idea to stride off without glancing back at her.

Charlie sat with her hands clutching her boots as she watched him walk away. For the first time since she'd left England, she began to think that her lifelong yearning for adventure had been a huge mistake. How could she have ever imagined, that she could step out of her secure, careful and predictable life in a misty, green island where the sun is as gentle as the rain and cope on her own in a harsh, unfriendly wilderness at the bottom of the globe?

She'd been worried about conning Matt, but was she also conning herself? On her first morning, she'd made one mistake after another. And now, she'd been stupid enough to offer herself as live bait to a crocodile!

During the long ride back to the stock camp, she remained doubtful, shaken and confused. It wasn't just her lucky escape from danger that shook her. Matt Lockhart disturbed her, too. He had an open-hearted honesty about him, as if he faced life fair and square, and that made her feel extra guilty about her deception. Added to that, he was far too good-looking. She certainly hadn't expected her boss to make her think about...

No! She shook her head. She wasn't thinking about anything except the job to be done.

Once they arrived at the camp, there was too much to do to keep worrying. They deposited their saddles and bridles in the shed and let their horses go in a grassy paddock after washing their backs and giving them a small feed of grain.

And they still had the huge job of drafting the cattle. The steers had to be separated from the heifers and the cows from their calves.

Throughout the rest of the afternoon, Matt barked instructions above the bellowing and snorting from the animals and the coaxing and cursing of the men. The ringers worked the metal swing gates sending the beasts into different holding pens.

Charlie's job was to perch atop the timber fence near Matt and to keep score of how many steers and heifers there were. She found it required intense concentration and she was glad to put aside memories of the unfortunate series of mishaps that seemed to have dogged her since she arrived at Sundown.

Despite the suffocating dust stirred up by the trampling hooves, she was happy to be focused on work again until finally, when the light fell out of the sky and night descended, the day's work was done.

It took all Charlie's energy to down the tasty camp stew before crawling into her swag. At last she'd stopped thinking about Matt, who had disappeared somewhere to consult with the helicopter pilots. She drifted straight into exhausted sleep.

But he came to her in her dreams…

He stood watching her as she walked out of an expanse of cool water, its surface sparkling with flashes of sunlight. Her hair was no longer brown, but blond again and it streamed over her shoulders. Her skin glistened sleekly wet, as she glided slowly, cat-like towards him. And he was looking at her as a man looks at a woman he wants.

His brown eyes, shadowed by desire, lingered, as if he was committing to memory the shape and texture of her breasts, her hips and her thighs. Tall, dark and strong, he stood, feet spread wide apart, with his gaze riveted on her.

"I want to make love to every delectable inch of you, Charlie Bell," he said with a slow, sexy smile.

And she'd never felt so desirable, so needy...

A rattling motor rudely interrupted the scene. The generator shattered the slumbering silence of the predawn and Charlie squinted sleepily as lights in the cook's wagon flickered on.

Morning again.

From the swags nearby, she heard muffled grunts of complaint and was relieved that at least she wasn't the only one who could have done with more sleep. Still, determined to make a good start, she jumped up quickly.

Half dazed, she joined the breakfast circle with her pannikin of tea and a plate of sausages and egg. It wasn't until after she'd sleepily plonked herself down on a log near the cook's fire that she discovered she was sitting beside Matt. With a jolt, the dream replayed in her head in vivid, shocking detail. *I want to make love to every delectable inch of you, Charlie Bell.*

"Sleep OK?" he asked her.

She knew she blushed! Like creeping fire, the warmth spread up her neck and into her cheeks. Matt's brown eyes seemed to be following its journey. Thank heavens he couldn't read her mind.

"I was dead to the world," she said, before taking a swig of her tea.

Another ringer joined the circle and, to let him in, Matt moved closer to Charlie. The length of his thigh, from hip to knee, pressed against her and Charlie nearly fell off the log. She couldn't believe her body's reaction. It was more overwhelming and embarrassing than her first teenage crush.

But she was twenty-seven years old now and she was going back to England in a few weeks to pick out a husband from her father's line-up. Maybe the sunshine had affected her hormones? Cooked her brains?

"Er—um—will we be doing yard work all day today?" she asked.

Matt nodded. "Actually," he said after a moment's thought. "We might get you to keep the crush full of calves. You won't yell and curse and frighten them the way the men do."

He smiled at her and for just a moment, Charlie fancied she saw a flash of special interest—the kind of interest he'd shown in the dream.

Enough!

She finished her breakfast quickly and stood. Deliberately switching her attention from her boss to the bush beyond the camp, she watched the pink rim in the eastern sky warm into orange. Her artistic eye liked what it saw. The landscape was peaceful and lovely at this early hour—the trees, grass and plain emerged—green, gold and silver with soft, olive green shadows.

But she didn't have long to stand idly admiring the scenery. Soon the day's work started. In the yard, calves were hauled roughly onto their sides and the process of branding, ear-marking, vaccinating and castrating began. Amidst the noise and the dust and the hiss of the branding iron, Charlie's job was to keep the single race full of calves, as well as making sure that the syringes were full of vaccine and the knife well washed in a tin of disinfectant.

Working as a team, they had to deal with each calf in less than a minute. And to Charlie's relief, the men accepted her. They no longer seemed to notice she was female, or from the other side of the world. They were too busy. They didn't bother to tease her and she was able to enjoy the sheer satisfaction of hard, physical work.

The best part of the job came at the end of the long day when Charlie was delegated the task of releasing the calves back into the paddock to join their mothers.

And she was pleased that she had enough energy left to take full advantage of the hot shower set up at the back of the shed. The previous night all she'd managed was a quick clean-up, but now she washed her hair and cleaned her nails and scrubbed off every trace of the day's dirt. And after her shower, she tossed her filthy jeans into a flour drum of sudsy water to soak along with the men's.

She was standing in the late-afternoon sunshine, brushing out her clean hair, when Matt walked up to her, looking just a little self-conscious. She hadn't seen much of him at all during the day.

"Can we talk?" he asked abruptly.

"I guess so," came her wary answer. She hoped she wasn't in trouble.

He led her some distance away from the camp and continued strolling slowly as he spoke. "I suppose you're very tired. It's been a long day."

A fresh breeze lifted her hair and cooled the back of her neck and she told him honestly, "I feel much better than I did last night. I must be getting used to the work."

"That's good." He paused and kicked at a tuft of grass with his boot.

Charlie stopped walking and looked at him curiously. "What did you want to tell me?"

"I wanted to ask you—"

"Yes?"

He let out his breath—half a laugh, half a sigh, shoved his hands into his pockets and threw his head back to stare at the late-afternoon sky.

Whatever he had to say was difficult to get out. Charlie felt panic flutter in her chest. "What have I done wrong now?"

His eyes met hers. "If we were in the city, I think I'd seriously consider asking you out on a date."

Oh! This was the last thing she expected. Charlie's heart pounded. "That would have been nice," she said softly.

"You know, to dinner or the theatre."

"Yes." She had a sudden vision of how it would be—

going into a restaurant with Matt. He would look tall and suntanned and splendid and she would wear silk—something elegant and—and very sexy.

She thought of her dream.

Matt looked around him at the rough camp, the dusty yards and the plains beyond and he grinned. "This isn't exactly a good scenario for dating, but there is a place nearby I'd like to show you." His eyes found hers again and he smiled shyly. "Seeing you're out here to catch a bit of the country."

Charlie's heart skipped and when he smiled like that, she forgot to be careful and her response was automatic. "I'd love to see it."

"Saddle up Duchess and let's go."

Like naughty teenagers sneaking away from a party, they collected their horses and galloped away from the camp. As they rode, Matt pointed to a row of red cliffs some distance away and together they raced across the plain towards it. Duchess snorted with delight and Charlie laughed aloud. Both she and the mare loved the thrill of gathering speed and open space.

The wall of rock, when they reached it, was smoothly sculpted, having been shaped and creviced by centuries of wind and rain. They dismounted and tied up their horses and Matt led Charlie through a narrow cleft in the rocks. The path wound its way between tall boulders and then the land suddenly opened out into paradise. They stood on a rocky ledge at the mouth of a deep cave and nearby, a waterfall tumbled into a deep pool of clear, green water.

Charlie drew in an admiring breath. "This *is* beautiful."

"I like it," he said simply. "In fact, I think it's the nicest place in the whole world." He took her hand. "Come and sit over here and watch the show."

Silently, Charlie settled beside him on the flat, sun-warmed rock, inexplicably happy to have him hold her hand and share this special place with her. It was just on dusk and as they watched, hundreds of birds flew in. Matt told Charlie their names—magpie geese, pygmy geese, finches and brolgas.

She let out a soft squeak of excitement as kangaroos and pretty-faced wallabies appeared, hopping silently down the rocks to the water's edge and dipping forward to peck at the water in a manner similar to the birds.

"I come here to be happy," Matt told her.

"I can understand that," Charlie murmured, her heart swelling with emotion. "Thank you so much for sharing it with me. I don't think I've ever had such a lovely surprise on a date." On impulse, she leant forward and pressed her lips to a patch of warm, brown skin just at the side of his mouth. Then unable to resist, she kissed him full on the lips.

She drew back. "Oops! That just seemed like the natural thing to do. I hope you don't mind."

He chuckled. "I was just getting around to something nice and natural like that myself." He pulled her close against his broad shoulder and one hand came up to cup her chin. With his open mouth, he traced the outline of her lips. "The problem is, Charlie," he murmured, his voice low and raspy, "once I start kissing you, I'm afraid it won't stop there."

"Let's worry about one thing at a time," Charlie surprised herself by saying and she sank against this beautiful man, while her body felt as if it was turning to liquid.

Leaning forward, he sipped at her lower lip, and she shivered with delight. He smiled. "I've been wanting to taste that lip ever since I first saw you."

"Even when you were mad at me?"

"Yeah," he grinned. "Especially then."

She grinned back and lifted her face, offering her mouth for him to explore and to her intense delight, it was exactly what he did.

His hands gently held her shoulders and his mouth slanted over hers. With easy confidence, he laid claim to her lips, touched his tongue to hers and delved the warm secrets of her mouth. He tasted as clean and fresh as the water that tumbled over the red rocks beside them and he smelled of sunlight and leather. Charlie threaded her fingers into his rough, soft hair. Every part of him felt very, very good.

His hands tenderly caressed her breasts and, like a string of firecrackers, every erogenous zone in her body caught alight. She felt breathless and totally out of control.

When finally they drew apart, she touched trembling fingers to her lips. "Wow! I've heard that Australian men are the best kissers in the world—"

He smiled slowly, his eyes, drowsy with desire. "Now you know it's true."

"Indeed I do."

"I've heard that English girls are very prim and proper."

"Really?" Charlie laughed before pursing her mouth into a tight-lipped, prim little circle.

"Aren't all English girls brought up to be ladies?"

"*Ladies?*" she echoed in a voice that suddenly shook. She bolted upright. For just a moment she thought Matt was setting a trap—about to unearth her real identity.

But he was tugging her close. "Don't worry, Charlie," he growled huskily. "I don't need a lady. I want someone like you—all woman."

He lowered his head to kiss her again, but for Charlie, the magic of the evening was suddenly slipping through her fingers. Her happiness was dissolving and disappearing like sugar in hot water.

Matt's innocent words reminded her that she was a fake. A big fat fraud. Not an ordinary English girl—an adventuring backpacker, who liked the bush life—but Lady Charlotte Bellamy. An earl's only daughter—with all the responsibility that entailed. And in the twenty-first century, it mostly entailed an enormous financial burden.

How on earth had she allowed herself to exchange breathtaking kisses with Matt when she knew he was out of her territory? It wasn't his fault. For all he knew there was nothing to stop them getting close, even getting serious and planning a future together. Closing her eyes, she silently cursed her rotten luck. Here was the most desirable man she'd ever met, but she couldn't let him begin to fall in love with her.

Matt's beautiful, tempting mouth touched hers again and with the greatest effort, she pulled away. It was time to be strong. Deceiving her parents by having this adventure was bad enough, but deceiving Matt—falling thoughtlessly into a highly unsuitable romantic entanglement—that was completely out of the question.

"What's the matter?" Matt looked puzzled, as if he couldn't understand her reaction. And Charlie couldn't blame him for being confused. Minutes earlier, she'd been leading him on shamelessly.

She edged a little further away on the rocky ledge. "Er—this—this discussion about ladies," she began hesitantly.

With a playful grin, he reached for her. "I was only teasing—"

She placed a restraining hand on his arm. "I know, but it—it reminded me that I should be thanking you for letting me ride Duchess."

"I beg your pardon?"

She rolled her eyes towards the darkening sky, feeling foolish and sad, because she wanted him to go on kissing her and knew that she mustn't be so weak. She tried to explain, waving her hands in the air as if to make the point clearer. "Ted Smith told me that you've given up your favourite mare for me. He said you always ride Duchess."

"The hell he did!" Suddenly Matt looked furious. A red tinge crept along his cheekbones and his eyes glinted darkly. "It's none of his flaming business."

Now Charlie felt worse than ever. She'd been trying to wriggle out of hot water and had landed Ted there instead.

She jumped to her feet. "I have a dreadful case of foot-in-mouth disease. Please, Matt, I didn't mean to get Ted into trouble."

He rose also and pulled her gently towards him. "Foot-in-mouth?" he murmured. "Now that's an interesting notion." With his big hands spread wide on her hips, he held her hard against him.

Lord, he felt good.

"As I was saying before, Charlie Bell, you have the most gorgeous mouth." He dropped tiny kisses first on her top lip and then her lower lip.

Oh, dear! He was so sexy. Of their own accord, her lips drifted apart once more and she wanted desperately to feel his kiss deepen. How weak she was! Groaning softly, she turned her head away. "I guess we should remember this is only a first date."

His eyebrows drew together and he swept his hands out to the sides, clear away from her. "Of course," he said with a frown.

"Thank you so much for bringing me here, Matt. It really is very special." Good heavens, now she sounded like she was reciting some polite little courtesy her nanny had taught her.

A ghost of a smile flickered across his features and she knew he was puzzled, perhaps hurt, by her sudden rejection. "We'd better get back," he said quietly. "You must be tired."

He'd picked up on her cue and was doing the right thing—acting like a gentleman, dropping any hint of romance. Her spirits plummeted.

She should be pleased.

Of course she was pleased.

She *had* to be pleased.

Without another word, Matt took her hand and led her back through the tunnel in the rocks to the horses. In silence they mounted and, cantering across the darkened plains, they returned to the camp.

CHAPTER FOUR

RAISED voices woke Charlie next morning. A cluster of men gathered near the cook's fire. She heard an angry shout and as she squinted through the early dawn light, she fancied she saw clenched fists being raised and shaken in threatening gestures.

Forgetting how tired she was after a wretched, sleepless night, she rolled out of her swag, hauled on her boots and hurried in her crumpled T-shirt and jeans to join the circle of onlookers. Ted Smith was glaring at a grim-faced Matt, his squinted eyes filled with malice and his face dark with fury.

Matt's gaze darted to Charlie as she approached. For brief seconds his fierce eyes held hers, then shot away again. His big shoulders rose and fell in time with his harsh breathing and, after a cursory glance at Ted Smith, he turned and strode away from them without speaking.

Alarmed, Charlie watched Matt's angry retreating back and then she swung back to Ted. His pale eyes regarded her with such contempt that she felt her face grow warm. He opened his mouth as if he wanted to say something, but another man grabbed his arm and pulled him roughly. "Give it a miss, Ted. You've already said enough to cost you your job."

A surge of adrenaline-charged guilt drenched Charlie. "Lost his job?" she echoed. Surely she hadn't landed the ringer in trouble by talking to Matt about Duchess?

There was no response, except some embarrassed shuffles from the circle of onlookers. Charlie scanned the group searching for eye contact with someone—anyone. They all stared at the ground. Desperate, she dashed after Matt.

"Matt!" she called.

But he kept walking.

"What's going on?"

He whipped around and his eyes flashed a warning when he saw her so close behind him. "Don't worry about it," he snapped. "Get your breakfast."

He *was* angry with her. "Please, Matt, I didn't want to get Ted into trouble."

Looking a touch embarrassed, he hesitated before muttering. "It was just a bit of a barney. Ted doesn't know when to shut his trap."

"But you're upset."

"Yeah." His jaw squared stubbornly.

"What did he say?"

To her frustration, he merely scowled and shook his head, keeping his lips tightly sealed.

"Ted looks like he's angry with me," she added.

Matt sighed and shrugged. "I told you, don't bother about it. It's a bloke thing. Ted flapped his jaws once too often and I took exception to his choice of descriptive language."

"About me?" Charlie persisted.

His face darkened and screwed into a grimace. "Damn it. I guess you'll hear something about it sooner or later. Our absence last night was noted by Ted and a couple of others. Tongues wag."

Charlie, just as the men had minutes earlier, stared at the dusty toes of her riding boots.

"But you can rest assured your reputation has been protected, Charlie. And Ted won't be around to make any more unsavoury comments."

"You've sacked him?"

"This isn't the first time Ted's made a nuisance of himself. He's crossed me one too many times, so he's lucky all he lost is his job." He clenched his fist. "He could easily be minus a few teeth."

"But—but I thought you needed every hand you can get at the moment."

With the briefest of smiles and another shrug of his broad shoulders, Matt said, "You'll just have to work that little bit harder, won't you?" He turned and continued walking away.

Charlie dropped her head into her hands. Last night she'd hurt Matt and now he'd taken his feelings out on Ted. Her presence was causing trouble.

What a weak fool she'd been. Yesterday, as soon as Matt mentioned the word "date," the warning bells should have rung loud and clear. But she'd been too busy admiring his physique and his cute smile. And then...she'd been carried away by how he looked at her... All her serious intentions had been forgotten.

In an effort to redeem herself over the next few days, she kept the lowest profile possible. She joined in the muster of another mob of cattle. This time she went with Arch and she worked with him in the yards as well. She saw little of Matt. He was busy dealing with the huge road trains that came in to take cattle to the markets on the coast and he left the mustering team to get on with their job. And that suited her.

But she missed him.

On the evening before they were due to leave the mustering camp and return to the homestead, he turned up again. Charlie saw him as he stepped out of the makeshift shower. Dressed only in jeans, his torso was bare and still just a little damp. As he walked, towelling his hair dry, dappled sunlight filtered through the overhead trees and played on the moving muscles in his smooth brown back, shoulders and arms. She couldn't help sneaking a good, long look.

"Hey, watch where you're going!"

She walked bang into Arch, who was sitting under a tree cleaning his saddle.

"Sorry," she muttered, blushing fiercely.

Arch's sceptical glance took in her red face and Matt's state of undress. He rolled his eyes, grunted and shook his head. But he said nothing.

Bursting with embarrassment, Charlie hurried off to the horse paddock and stayed there for ages while she gave Duchess the most thorough rub-down of her life.

The next day the team returned to Sundown homestead. For two nights they were to stay there before they began the next muster on another section of the vast property. For two nights they could sleep back in the ringers' quarters—on proper beds.

Charlie was surprised to discover that everyone ate the evening meals together with Matt in the homestead kitchen. The ringers relaxed and enjoyed a few beers with their meal.

Halfway through the noisy first course, Charlie couldn't help asking her neighbour, "Does the boss always eat with his workers?"

The young ringer pulled a face. "I guess so." He frowned. "What's so strange about that?"

"It's not strange—just different," she replied. "My father wouldn't dream of eating with his servants."

Suddenly the conversation around the table stopped. Curious heads turned in her direction and Charlie felt as if she'd been shoved under a microscope.

"Does your dad have many servants?" Arch asked cautiously.

Her heartbeats suddenly doubled their pace. "No, no," she answered hastily. "I—didn't say servants, did I? I meant *staff*. My father's a bit old-fashioned."

Arch frowned as if he wasn't satisfied with her answer.

"What's your old man do?" someone else asked.

"He's an art collector and dealer." She avoided eye contact with Arch.

"Sounds posh. What about you, Charlie? You work in stables?"

"Sometimes."

From the far end of the table, Matt was also watching Charlie and he seemed to be listening very carefully to the conversation. Remembering the glowing account of her experience with horses that she'd supplied in her job application, she felt as if she walked on eggshells.

"You know anything about art?" Arch surprised her by asking.

She didn't like the suspicious glint in his eyes. "A little," she hedged. "You can't grow up with an art fanatic like my father without some of it rubbing off."

Another ringer chimed in with enthusiasm, "You should take a look at the boss's paintings."

"Really?" Charlie's fork clattered onto her plate. She looked down the table to Matt. "You're an art collector?"

"He's an artist," someone supplied.

Matt gave a self-deprecating shrug. "It's just a hobby. I'm a Sunday painter." He looked as if he would like the conversation to end.

"Don't be modest, Matt," the man next to him cut in. "You're bloody good." He turned in Charlie's direction. "If you know anything about pictures, Charlie, you should have a look and tell him how good he is."

"I'd love to see them sometime," Charlie murmured softly. She stared at her plate as she took in this startling news. She felt sorry for Matt, being put on the spot like that. And it could be embarrassing, if she looked at his paintings and found they were awful. What would these Outback ringers know about Art with a capital A? Would she be able to find the right tactful things to say?

As the ringers filed out of the kitchen at the end of the meal, Matt stepped forward and touched her lightly on the arm, but he might have poked her with an electric cattle prod, the way she reacted. She spun around and gasped loudly to find him so close.

"Can you wait a moment?" he asked.

Silently, she nodded.

And they waited, taking care not to look at each other, while the men cleared the room. At last they were on their own and Matt's dark eyes searched her face while his Adam's apple moved in his throat.

"You'd like to show me your paintings?" she asked.

His face creased into a brief grin. "Isn't that a line old lechers use to lure young maidens to their rooms?"

Charlie's chest tightened. "So the story goes."

He ran strong fingers through his thick dark hair and Charlie watched the movement, remembering how surprisingly soft his hair had felt when she'd done that.

"I don't really expect you to look at my stuff," he said quickly. "But I did wonder if you know enough to recognise a good painting if you happen to stumble on one."

She dropped her gaze to the floor and held her hands in front of her, palms pressed together as she considered the best way to answer. She didn't want to tell Matt about her high-powered job at one of London's top galleries. That would make him far too suspicious. "My parents live, talk and breathe art. I've picked up quite an extensive knowledge." She looked at his big hands and tried to imagine them holding an artist's brush.

When her gaze met his once more, she was surprised to see the tension in his face. This is important to him, she thought with faint alarm. "I'd really love to see your work," she added, accompanying her words with an encouraging smile.

"OK." He shrugged, and led her into the homestead's main lounge room. "But you don't have to be gentle with me. I don't expect you to be impressed."

But Charlie was impressed. Mightily impressed.

She walked into the centre of the room and stopped, open-mouthed. In an unconscious gesture of astonishment, her hands crossed over her heart as she circled slowly on the spot, her eyes riveted to the walls. "Matt! These are sensational."

Behind her, Matt stood watching her with his thumbs hooked through the belt loops in his jeans.

Charlie stopped rotating to pay closer attention to a large canvas—a study of a stockman leaning on slip-rails at the end of a hard day's work in the yard. "The colour," she whispered. "The way you've captured the Australian sunlight." She shook her head and spun on her heel again to take in some more paintings. "And your style—it's unique. You manage to tell so much with just a few bold strokes. You've combined a contemporary, sophisticated feel with something that's almost primitive—primeval—like the land itself. This stuff is brilliant!"

"Glad you like them," he said simply.

"You must have had some training?"

"At boarding school, I had a good art teacher, who was big on technique. I've just gone on from there by myself."

Suddenly Charlie hurried forward to look more closely at a small painting—bright red slashes of rock contrasting with deep green water and an astonishing blue sky. She called back to him over her shoulder. "This is the waterhole you took me to the other day."

"Yeah." In a few long strides he crossed the room to stand behind her.

Charlie could feel him close to her back and fine hairs rose on her skin. Tears pricked her eyes. Heavens! She'd been trying so hard to feel nothing for Matt. And now, suddenly she was feeling *everything!* Overwhelming admiration, shameless lust and longing...*love?*

She turned to face him and she knew he would see the diamond-bright tears in her eyes, the trembling of her lips as she struggled to smile. It was too hard to be strong and resist his charms. He was so beautiful. His paintings were just an extension of the man—incredibly beautiful and bursting with vitality. Unique.

"I love them, Matt," she whispered.

"Good," was all he said, holding her in his warm gaze

and stepping closer till his body nudged hers, edging her backwards. His hands came to rest on the wall on either side of her.

"I'm sorry—" she began, but her words were cut off as he lowered his head and kissed her hard and long.

And once more, Charlie felt she was dissolving into a mass of warm sensations...falling under his spell...losing her grip on common sense.

But how could a girl be sensible when Matt's divine lips and tongue urged her to forget about her parents and England and to simply let her feelings take over?

"Matt," she murmured, in what was supposed to be an attempt to stop this madness.

His mouth roamed along her jaw and she arched her neck, eager for more. His hands came off the wall and, spreading wide, spanned her ribs.

"Oh, dear," she whispered feebly, placing her hands over his, but showing no resistance as they moved towards her breasts.

A low sound growled in his throat as his hands moulded her shape through her blouse. "Charlie, Charlie," he whispered, through his kiss.

Any minute now, she'd give in. To resist Matt's loving was asking too much of any woman. With a last-ditch effort at self-control, she thrust her hands into the middle of his chest and pushed him back. "We mustn't."

But, bless him, he seemed determined to persuade her otherwise. "Couldn't this count as a second date?"

Charlie's lips curled in a wan smile as she held him away from her. "Matt Lockhart, why aren't you old and balding and grey? I didn't come to the Outback to go on dates with my boss."

"But it's not a bad idea." His hands slid lower, till they were slowly massaging her backside.

She tried to ignore how good it felt. "I've already caused

problems with Ted. I made a mistake coming here, allowing you to think I was a man when you hired me—''

"I'm beginning to think the best mistake I ever made was hiring you." Leaning closer again, he nuzzled the side of her neck just below her ear.

"But you don't know anything about me."

"We can change that in a flash," he murmured seductively. "Wouldn't you like to get better acquainted?"

A sob of despair burst from Charlie's lips. She had no self-control in his arms. Once more she let him kiss her and she kissed him back, their mouths seeking each other's hungrily. Passion matched passion as they urged their bodies tight together, desperate to discover every last detail.

He hitched her higher so that the very centre of her longing wedged hard against his and she moved against him in a blatant act of desire. Oh, Lord, this feels right, she thought.

But it isn't right!

It can never be right!

Stop now!

From somewhere in the dim depths of her consciousness, the reprimand shouted and tormented her. In a haze of despair, she went still in his arms, stopped returning his kisses, and sadly slid lower till her feet reached the floor again.

"What's the matter?"

"Everything!" she cried, blinking back tears. She touched his cheek, feeling the strong line of his cheekbone. "I'm sorry, Matt."

And this time he didn't interrupt. His eyes locked onto hers, deadly serious, on the edge of anger.

"I'd love to get to know you better—" she stammered. "But, under the circumstances, I don't think it's wise."

"What do you mean?" he challenged. "What circumstances?"

" I'm—I'm not looking for a holiday affair."

"I wasn't exactly looking for this, either," he protested. "But, crikey—who knows? Perhaps we're meant to have something bigger than a passing affair.'' Once more his hands firmly clasped her hips. He held her in front of him and studied her face intently, his eyes still searching hers as if he would find the answer he needed there.

Charlie returned his gaze, hoping he could read in her eyes the message that she dared not speak. *I'd give anything to stay here and love you.*

''You're the most beautiful woman I've ever met, Charlie. And I thought you felt the way I do—''

She pressed her fingers over his lips. ''I happen to find you very—*very* attractive. But let's—let's think it over some more before we get carried away.'' Smiling sadly, she added, ''You really do tempt a girl, Mr. Lockhart.''

Then, taking a deep breath, she turned back to the painting of the waterhole. ''I really love this.''

He whirled around, glaring at the painting, and taking advantage of his distraction, Charlie hastily slipped away, out of his arms, out of the room. Down the hallway she stumbled and onto the veranda, then across the dirt road to the ringers' hut.

She heard him call her once, but she didn't turn back.

And he didn't come after her.

Matt was gone the next morning.

At breakfast, Charlie didn't dare ask where he was. Everyone's attention was taken by two young professional rodeo riders who'd turned up looking for work between competitions. Charlie ate quietly and left early. But as she stepped out of the kitchen, Arch Grainger was waiting on the veranda.

''Charlie, can you spare a minute?''

Her heart thudded guiltily as she followed Matt's head stockman to a quiet spot at one end of the veranda. Was she going to get a lecture?

While his mouth remained fixed in a grim, downward

curve, he offered her a seat in an old wicker chair and sat opposite her.

"How can I help you?" she asked as calmly as she could.

"You can be honest with me, Miss Bell."

Her heart began to boom like a bass drum. "What about?"

He flattened his lips into a grimacing smile. "I know there's more to you than meets the eye. I don't know what your secret is, but I know you've got one."

Sitting ramrod straight, Charlie gripped the arms of her chair. Arch didn't seem to expect an outright admission from her, so she remained silent, dreading where this conversation was heading.

Arch leant forward, resting his elbows on his knees, and continued, "I also know you and Matt only had to take one look at each other and there were more bells and whistles going off than in a circus parade."

Feeling wretched, she dropped her gaze.

"You probably think this is none of my business and I guess you're right. But we both know you'll be leaving soon, Charlie, and I just hope whatever's happening here between the two of you doesn't hurt you, or the bloke I love more than a son."

After two sleepless, guilt-ridden nights, Charlie's nerves were too fragile to survive this direct hit. Without warning, her eyes filled with tears that spilled and tumbled onto her cheeks.

Arch immediately looked distressed. Clumsily, he tried to pat her shoulder. "I'm sorry, love. Don't take too much notice of me sticking my beak in."

But he'd exposed a raw nerve—the very thing she'd been worrying about all night long. While she stayed here on Sundown, she and Matt would go on wanting each other, till eventually things got out of hand. Some amazing chemistry was at work between them, lighting a fire that threatened to burn out of control. But neither of them would be happy with a one-night stand.

And Arch was right. She did have a secret that could only hurt Matt.

At the other end of the veranda, the kitchen fly-screen door banged open and the two rodeo riders stepped out. The answer to this dilemma was being presented to her on a plate. Charlie's mind was made up in an instant.

"Don't worry, Arch," she said sniffling away the last of her tears. "I don't want to upset your boss any more than you do. I came here for an uncomplicated, exciting, Outback adventure, but things are getting more complicated every day, so I'll head off now." She nodded in the direction of the men. "You've got two replacements for Ted and me. And the mail truck's due in this morning. I can be gone before Matt gets back."

Arch looked worried. "I didn't want to scare you that bad," he said.

"You're talking common sense." Charlie pushed herself out of the chair. "Wish Matt all the best for me. I'm sure these new fellows will be much more use to him than I am and tell him that it's all for the best that I'm leaving now."

"Perhaps you should wait and see him first," Arch suggested, clearly uncomfortable with this sudden turn of events.

But Charlie knew that if she saw Matt again, she would weaken. She would throw herself into his arms and end up in an even bigger mess.

She moved away. "This is how it's got to be Arch," she mumbled as tears threatened again, and turning swiftly, she jumped down the low veranda steps and dashed back to her room to pack her things.

"What do you mean, Charlie's gone? How the hell can she be gone?" Matt roared.

Arch flung down his hat and shoved his hands on his hips.

"Those two rodeo fellows arrived here looking for work and Charlie got a bee in her bonnet about how they would be better on the job than she would." He gave a helpless little shrug. "And she took off."

"When did she leave?"

"Yesterday morning."

"Didn't you try to stop her?"

"She was very determined."

A wary glint in Arch's eye alerted Matt's suspicions. "You said something to her, didn't you?"

"What about?"

"How the hell do I know? But I bet you frightened her off." Matt spun on his heel and paced down the veranda.

He couldn't believe Charlie was gone. The gaping hole in his gut at the thought of never seeing her again burned like crazy. He'd never been so bewitched by a woman. Beautiful, gutsy and passionate. He'd hadn't ever expected to meet someone like her—certainly not out here. Of course, he knew there'd been something bothering her, but given time, surely they could sort everything out?

Striding into his den, he reached his desk and sorted wildly through the pile of papers there. At last he found what he wanted—the Sydney phone number he'd rung when he hired her. He had to get to the bottom of this.

His call was answered on the third ring. "Hello, Sarah Bellamy."

"Good afternoon. Matt Lockhart here."

"Oh, Mr. Lockhart!"

"You know why I'm ringing?"

"Um—er—you're looking for Charlie?"

"Exactly. Where is she?"

"On a plane heading for England."

Matt cursed loudly and almost threw the telephone at the wall.

"I'm sorry, Mr. Lockhart. She didn't tell me much. Just

that things didn't work out.'' Sarah Bellamy paused and then added, ''She seemed dreadfully upset.''

''Can you give me her address in England?''

There was a definite hesitation on the other end of the line.

''She lives in Derbyshire, doesn't she?'' Matt's mind raced, searching for an excuse to contact her. ''I need to send her pay.''

''Oh, I see. Her parents have a place in Derbyshire and as she's still officially on holidays, my guess is that's where she'll be.'' There was another moment of hesitation. ''I suppose it won't hurt to give you their address.''

He snatched up a pen and recorded the details of Charlie Bell's home in England.

CHAPTER FIVE

MATT zipped his leather jacket against the biting English wind and stared at the scribbled address on the smudged and creased paper in his hand, but he didn't really need to check it, he knew every detail by heart. He looked again at the huge wrought-iron gates in front of him. The name on the paper was the same as that on the brass nameplate—Greenfields.

But there had to be a mistake.

These gates led up a long, sweeping, gravelled drive to an enormous stately home. Charlie Bell wouldn't live here!

He checked his map, to make sure that he'd followed the correct route out of Derby, but, no, he hadn't taken any wrong turns. Frowning, he surveyed the grounds inside the gates. There was a lush, green park, a circular pond and a grand old house, three storeys high.

Struth! Sarah had mentioned that Charlie's parents had property, but he'd no idea it was an estate like this! He'd pictured her home as a quaint English farmhouse with roses over the door, a few fields dotted with fat sheep and separated by stone walls. He couldn't imagine the Charlie he knew living in a mansion like this.

But there was only one way to find out. Straddling his hired motorbike, he kicked it into action and headed up the drive to Greenfields.

Chasing off to England to find Charlie had been an enormous gamble. For weeks he'd held off and then finally Arch had given him a king-sized lecture.

"Listen, mate. I'm sick and tired of you snapping and snarling at everyone's heels. You've been kicking doors and mopin' around ever since Charlie left. If one of our bulls

156

was acting like you are, I'd either shoot him or cut the fencing wire and let him have his way.'' He'd poked an angry finger into Matt's chest. "I can't very well shoot you, so consider the bloody fence cut.''

And then he'd pulled a suitcase from under the table and dumped it at Matt's feet. "The mustering's taken care of. Here's your bag and here's your passport. Go, buy a ticket to flaming England.''

And now, here he was—roaring to a halt at the bottom of low stone steps, that led to an imposing front door. His gaze raked his surroundings, taking note of the classic, uncluttered architecture of the house—straight lines, square corners and tall windows overlooking the park.

Best to get this over.

Matt raised a hand to the brass knocker, but the door opened before he could make a sound.

An elderly man stood before him. "G'day." Matt flashed a brave grin. "Do I have the pleasure of addressing Mr. Bell?''

The man frowned and his grey eyes narrowed. "There's no one of that name here, sir.''

"Oh," responded Matt. "What about a Miss Bell? Charlie Bell.''

His request was answered by another frown and a very definite shake of the head.

"Perhaps she works somewhere on the property," Matt suggested, trying to be helpful in case the old fellow's memory was unreliable. "Could she be in the stables? She's good with horses.''

Behind him on the gravel drive, the smooth grumble of an expensive engine drew closer. Over his shoulder, Matt saw a gleaming silver sports car glide to a stop.

A thin, blond man with a clipped moustache and wearing a formal tuxedo, uncurled from the driver's seat. Without so much as a glance in Matt's direction, he marched arrogantly across the drive, loped up the stairs and slapped his driving gloves and a woollen scarf into the man at the door's hands.

"Afternoon, Norton," he said with a brief nod, before disappearing into the house.

Matt gaped after him, then swung his gaze back to the old man, who was folding the discarded scarf neatly over his arm. "Norton?" he said. "Is that your name?"

"It is, sir."

Matt offered his hand. "Matt Lockhart. Pleased to meet you."

Norton accepted Matt's handshake with a polite smile.

"You're a butler?"

"That is correct." Norton glanced at his wristwatch. "I'm afraid I can't help you find this young woman you're searching for."

Matt frowned and sighed and lifted a suntanned hand to scratch his jaw. "Sarah Bellamy must have given me the wrong address."

Stepping forward, Norton peered at the much creased paper in Matt's hand. "Sarah Bellamy, sir?"

"Yeah," sighed Matt. "She's Charlie's cousin."

"Really?" Norton's grey eyes widened behind his wire-rimmed glasses. "Good heavens, I think perhaps you're at the right place after all." His tone was one of controlled shock.

At that moment, there was a tinkle of laughter in the hall behind Norton. Matt glimpsed a swish of emerald green as footsteps approached. The driver of the silver sports car re-emerged with a beautiful girl on his arm. She was dressed in an elegant, dark green velvet evening gown. Her soft, full lips were made dramatic by lipstick and her golden hair was upswept into a charming knot to reveal a long white neck. She was absolutely gorgeous.

She was Charlie.

Matt felt as if he'd stepped on a land mine. His body lurched and swayed, and his heart felt like it was exploding in his chest. He gaped at the vision before him—an exquisite, golden-haired, totally upmarket version of *his* Charlie.

With her arm looped through that of her escort, she stopped abruptly and stared at him. "Matt!"

It was like seeing her from a long way off as he watched the colour leach from her cheeks and her eyes widen in shock.

"Good heavens, Matt," she stammered.

"Surprise, surprise," he managed to reply.

She stared at him, her green eyes huge in her pale face, her mouth and chin trembling. The way she reached out as if to touch him seemed automatic, but she must have remembered she was still attached to the blond fellow. Turning to him, she began a stammering explanation. "Jeremy, this—this is Matt Lockhart. He owns Sundown, an enormous, wonderful cattle property in Australia. We met while I was out there. Matt, this is—Jeremy Groves."

As Matt remembered to offer his hand, the butler bent close and murmured in his ear, "*Lord* Jeremy Groves."

"Pleasure to meet you, Lockhart," responded Jeremy without warmth. "Look, old fellow, I'm terribly sorry to rush Charlotte away when you've just arrived, but we have tickets to the opera."

Matt held up his hand. "By all means, please go. Don't let me hold you up. I was just passing through the district and I thought I'd drop in—to say a quick hello to Char—Charlotte."

"Oh, Matt, I'm so sorry." Charlie slipped her arm away from Jeremy's and stepped towards him.

An exquisite perfume accompanied her and the low necked velvet dress exposed the pale slenderness of her throat and a tantalising hint of the perfection of her breasts. Her eyes were made lustrous by a watery sheen.

He blinked and did his best to swallow the iceberg-sized lump clogging his throat as he struggled to speak. "Nothing to apologise for. You had no idea I'd turn up out of the blue.''

''Charlotte, my dear,'' Jeremy urged, tugging at her arm. ''We're going to be late.''

Swinging a bewildered glance to her partner and then back to Matt, she asked him, in a soft breathy little voice, ''Are you staying nearby?''

Norton stepped forward. ''I can arrange accommodation for Mr. Lockhart at the Greenfield Motor Inn.''

''Oh,'' beamed Charlie, her face lighting up with a sudden, stunning brilliance that hit Matt like the blast of a laser. ''That's a super idea, Norton.'' And as Jeremy led her away, she called back over her shoulder, ''Better still, Norton, Matt can stay here. Get a room ready for him.''

''Very well,'' Norton responded, and Charlie beamed again and turned to hurry after Jeremy.

As Norton and Matt watched the sleek, silver car shoot down the drive, the butler spoke, ''It seems you've found your Charlie Bell, Mr. Lockhart.''

Matt shook his head. ''No, mate,'' he sighed. ''I'm afraid I've found someone completely different.''

Norton cleared his throat. ''Lady Charlotte Bellamy to be precise.''

For painful seconds, Matt stared at him. ''*Lady* Charlotte?'' he repeated. ''She's a lady? You mean, her father's a duke or something?''

''An earl.''

''Damn it to hell!'' Matt glared at the twin rear lights of Lord Groves's sports car as it whizzed through the front entry gates and his voice cracked as he turned to the old butler. ''What the blazes was she doing on my property masquerading as a ringer?''

Matt cursed again, under his breath this time, and he paced the doorstep and smashed the fist of one hand into the palm of the other.

Norton shook his head and cleared his throat uncomfortably. "Now, sir, unfortunately, Lady Charlotte's parents aren't at home this evening, but if you'll step this way, I'll show you to the sitting room and arrange a room for you for tonight."

"No way!" exclaimed Matt. "Sorry, Norton. I don't mean to be rude. Thanks for the offer, but I can't stay here."

Norton accepted this remark with a bow of the head. "Can I recommend the motor inn?"

"I think I'd be better to get clear out of the district. Coming here has been the most stupid mistake I've ever made."

"Mr. Lockhart," Norton pursed his lips thoughtfully, "I've known Lady Charlotte since she was just thirty minutes old. May I be so bold as to comment that I've never seen her look at *anyone* the way—" He paused and cleared his throat again. "Let me make a booking for you locally. It's too late to try to find accommodation anywhere else on a Friday evening."

Propped against the bar of the Greenfield Arms, Matt nursed a pint of ale and stared moodily at the flag stone floor. What an A-grade ass he'd made of himself. Matt Lockhart, nobody's fool, had stuffed things up in the most spectacular way possible.

Normally, he was a practical bloke, not at all prone to fantasy. So how the hell had he thought he could jump on a plane, wing his way across the globe and have Charlie immediately fall into his arms when he took her by surprise?

Throwing back his head, he downed his beer in a long swallow. For weeks now, he'd wasted hours and hours, thinking about her—remembering her taste. Fantasising about the smell and the feel of her. The way her eager mouth opened under his. Each memory made his body tighten unbearably.

And he'd been so sure he read her emotions correctly.

Something very strong had been developing between them. He'd never looked into another woman's eyes and

found her looking back at him with such warmth and soft-
ness and longing. He'd decided he needed to take the initia-
tive, or lose her forever.

What a disaster!

Elbows on the bar, he leaned his throbbing head into his
hands. What really ate at his heart now, was how she'd de-
ceived him. His lively, lovely Charlie had been replaced by
a vision of regal splendour—a dazzling, unattainable woman
from a totally different culture and lifestyle. Almost another
era.

What the blazes had she been up to on Sundown?

He ordered another pint and scowled as his gaze swept
the smoky, laughter-filled pub. It was time to think through
his options. Never in his life had he backed down or walked
away when things got tough.

He had no choice really. Tomorrow he'd front up to
Charlie and get the truth out of her. He'd take the bad news
on the chin. But he'd have his say, as well. Darn right he
would. He didn't take kindly to being fooled.

He remembered the square brown paper package he'd
nursed all the way from the other side of the world. Whatever the circumstances, she had to have it. Whatever else
tomorrow brought, this parcel was meant for Charlie and no
one else.

That was how it would happen. He would present his gift,
get his frustrations off his chest by telling her how damn
stupid her pretence had been and then walk clear out of her
life.

Back to the world Down Under where he belonged.

Nestling back into the soft leather of the passenger seat in
Jeremy's car, Charlie was glad to be going home at last.
She'd been rather poor company this evening. During the
entire performance of *Madame Butterfly,* she'd been thinking
about Matt.

The story unfolding on the stage had been about a

Japanese woman in love with an American, but her thoughts were absorbed by her own story of an English woman in love with an Australian. She hadn't really stopped thinking about him for the past month.

No matter where she went, who she met, what she did, on every occasion, Charlie found a reason to think about Matt Lockhart.

Jeremy's car swept up the drive to Greenfields and as soon as he pulled up, his hand slid along the back of the seat and, with a smug smile, he walked his fingers along Charlie's shoulders. For some reason, the gesture struck her as sleazy. Charlie suppressed a desire to wriggle away from his cool touch.

"Your parents are still in the Lakes District, aren't they?" he murmured, leaning closer.

"They'll be home tomorrow," she answered sharply.

"But not tonight," Jeremy persisted. He grazed her cheek with his lips and his moustache tickled her unpleasantly.

Charlie edged back slightly. "But my guest is staying here."

"That Australian fellow?"

"Yes."

"So what? He'll be sound asleep. We'll have the place to ourselves."

Why couldn't Jeremy be both more subtle and more attractive? Charlie suppressed a groan. How did he expect her to fall into his arms when Matt was here at Greenfields? Suddenly she knew it would be impossible to ask Jeremy inside.

"Matt will be jet-lagged," she suggested desperately. "He will probably be wide awake, waiting for his body clock to catch up." Her fingers fastened on the door handle and she pushed it down. To her relief, the door sprang open. "Thank you for a super evening." She favoured Jeremy with a dazzling smile as she slipped out of his car.

His reply was an open-mouthed gasp of astonishment.

This was their third date and he had been less than delicate in his hints that this evening they should progress to a more intimate relationship.

"Goodnight," she said, closing the passenger door firmly and raising a hand to wave.

But he didn't wave back. With an angry sniff, Jeremy accelerated down the drive, his tyres spinning, throwing up gravel.

Charlie didn't take time to brood over her escort's hurt feelings. With a light step and an even lighter heart she hurried into the house. As always, good old Norton was waiting up for her in his dressing gown and slippers. He enquired about the opera, but Charlie ignored the query. Grabbing his hands she demanded, "Is Matt asleep?"

"I've no idea," Norton surprised her by replying.

"Don't be silly, Norton," she cried, giving his hands an impatient shake. "Where is he? What room did you put him in? I've got to speak to him."

"But, Lady Charlotte, he's not here. He wouldn't stay."

She frowned. "What do you mean?"

"Mr. Lockhart seemed very upset. He's chosen to stay at the motor inn."

"Oh." Charlie slumped against the polished mahogany banister at the foot of the staircase. "That's that then," she said with a soft sigh.

"It is indeed," Norton agreed, and with the wisdom she knew to expect from him, he said no more on the matter.

Her eyes stung with sudden tears, impossible to hold back. "You think he seemed *very* upset?"

"I'm afraid so," came the gentle answer.

"Then I've got to ring him."

"But it's very late at night," Norton suggested. "I think it would be wiser to wait till morning."

She blinked back a tear or two.

"Shall I make you some supper?"

"No. No, Norton, thanks. I'll—I'll go straight to bed.

Goodnight.'' Not wanting Norton to see just how desperately miserable she was, Charlie turned and lifting her long velvet skirt high, ran up the stairs, wishing with all her heart that she could be Charlie Bell again.

She woke next morning feeling restless and edgy and her first thoughts were of Matt. He'd always been an early riser, so she decided to ring him straightaway. She couldn't bear to wait any longer to hear his voice.

Pulling on slacks and a soft rose coloured wool sweater, she ran downstairs to the telephone on the hall table. The wiring in her parents' house was so ancient they hadn't liked to risk overloading the system with bedside phones.

Anxiously, she thumbed through the pages of the telephone directory, located the number she wanted and dialled with a shaking finger.

''Good morning, Greenfields Motor Inn.''

A moment of blind panic hit Charlie. She was about to be connected to Matt and she hadn't given enough thought to what she wanted to say. Should she start with an apology?

''Could I speak to Mr. Lockhart, please?''

''I'm afraid Mr Lockhart has already left,'' the receptionist told her. ''He booked out half an hour ago.''

He's left? Stunned, Charlie stared at the receiver in her hand. But Matt couldn't have gone already! He couldn't leave without seeing her. They had to talk! ''Did he leave a forwarding address?'' she managed to ask.

''No, I'm sorry, he didn't.''

She'd lost him!

Feeling as if she'd been dropped from a great height, Charlie crashed the receiver down. She clutched at her stomach with one hand and rammed her other fist against her mouth to hold back noisy sobs of disappointment.

''Lady Charlotte.'' Norton's soft voice behind her brought her spinning 'round. ''Norton, he's gone!'' she cried and fell forward into her old friend's arms, unable to hold back the tears. "I wanted to apologise to him," she sobbed.

"There, there," he murmured in his soft, gentle voice, just as he had when she was little.

"I made a terrible mistake," she wailed into his shoulder. "When I was in Australia I—I—"

"Travelled incognito?" he suggested gently. "Pretended to be a simple, untitled girl called Charlie Bell?"

She nodded and rested her forehead against his thin, faithful chest. "I feel so guilty and confused," she whispered. For several minutes she stood, clinging to Norton, letting her misery dampen the front of his suit.

Matt had travelled all the way from Australia to see her. What a terrible way for him to learn about her deception! She couldn't blame him for being angry, for leaving straightaway. But oh, Lord! How could she bear it?

She clung to Norton and sobbed some more.

"Anybody home?" The voice with the Australian accent was distinctly recognisable.

Charlie's head jerked upwards and her teary eyes met Norton's twinkling grey gaze.

"There's someone at the door," he said with a knowing smile. Simultaneously, they hurried forward, Charlie swiping at her eyes with the backs of her hands.

Matt stood in the half-opened doorway, taking up most of the space. Under his arm, he carried a brown package. He looked tired, but quite, quite gorgeous.

Charlie's heart skated figures of eight in her chest and she doubted her ability to speak. She was grateful that Norton took over the greetings. "Good morning, Mr. Lockhart."

"Morning," replied Matt grimly. "I—er—wanted to drop this off." He held the package out in front of him and seemed to avoid looking at her.

"Certainly, sir," murmured Norton, taking the package carefully. "I'll attend to this."

Now Matt's gaze swung slowly to Charlie. In a surprisingly pale face, his dark, brown eyes were haunted and sad and she saw with a guilty start, just how deeply she had shocked him.

"That's for you," he said, nodding his head towards the package. "But you can look at it later. I just need to get one or two things off my chest and then I'll be out of here."

She tried to speak, but her throat was completely choked.

"Why don't you show Mr. Lockhart into the east room?" Norton suggested. "I'll bring through some tea and toast."

"Y-yes," Charlie stammered. "That's a good idea, Norton." Feeling like an invalid just recently let out of bed, she took a shaky step forward. "This way."

Somehow, she managed to walk the distance down the hall without her legs giving way. Once inside the big sunny living room, she clung to the arm of a chair while Matt strode the carpet with his hands in his pockets and his big leather jacket unzipped.

He looked around him, assessing the elegant antique furniture, the yellow wallpaper, the vases of fresh flowers and the tall French windows leading to a flagstone courtyard. For slightly longer, his gaze rested on the elegantly framed paintings…but she knew he wasn't here for a viewing of her father's art collection.

And now it seemed inappropriate to explain that this was one of the very few restored rooms in the entire house. Three quarters of Greenfields was boarded up, waiting till money was found for much needed renovations.

"I'm so sorry, Matt," she found the courage to say at last.

He stopped pacing. "That makes two of us."

"I didn't want to hurt you," she added, hoping desperately that he would believe her. "I can explain…"

Silently, he dipped his head, as if asking her to elaborate.

"I wanted an adventure—an Outback adventure," she began, keeping her hands stiffly at her sides. "But if I'd gone as Lady Charlotte, people would have found ways to shield me from the authentic Outback. I wanted a taste of the real thing and to be no one out of the ordinary.''

''You said you came to Australia to fulfil a dream.''

Charlie nodded cautiously. ''That's right.''

''That's why I came here—to fulfil a dream of my own.''

For a long moment, he didn't speak. Then he said softly, ''You see, there was a catch, you didn't bargain for. I fell in love with you.''

He said it so simply, so honestly, Charlie felt her stomach drop to her toes.

''And I think you knew it,'' Matt added as he slowly folded his arms across his chest and locked his gaze with hers. ''I don't make a habit of falling in love.''

''No, of course,'' she cried and took two faltering steps towards him, but he looked so stern, so tense that she stopped. What could she say? Ever since she'd set foot back in England, she'd been absolutely certain she loved him, too.

But there was her problem...

''Problem is,'' Matt continued in that hard, edgy voce she'd never heard him use before, ''I fell in love with an illusion.''

He ignored her small cry of protest.

''The woman I love isn't a titled lady with a stately home, a butler and an upper-crust boyfriend,'' he rushed on, as if he had to get everything out in a hurry. ''The girl I fell in love with is a free spirit, who'll tackle anything. A gutsy girl, who'll muster and yard cattle and whose reputation would be defended in fist fights, if necessary.'' He paused then added softly, ''That was Charlie Bell.''

Raising her eyes to meet his, Charlie tried to be brave. ''Matt, please understand I never meant to deceive you.''

''That's not true! You went out of your way to deceive me.''

She flinched. ''Well, yes, I guess I did plan the deception on one level—when I wanted that job and an Outback adventure, but on a *personal* level—when we—when I found out how I felt—how I felt about *you*—''

A heart-stopping, soft glow leapt into his eyes.

"I tried hard to resist you," she went on. "And I didn't want *you* to fall in love with Charlie—when she—when she didn't exist. Oh, Matt, I don't know what to do," she cried, stumbling towards him, tears streaming down her cheeks.

She wanted to dash headlong into his arms, but his rigid stance and the hard glitter that had returned to his eyes stopped her. Oh, how she wished he would haul her against him as he had in the past. Just one more hug, one more taste of his fabulous kisses...

There was a throat-clearing sound at the door.

Through her tears, Charlie looked past Matt's shoulder to see Norton holding a tray.

"Lord Groves has arrived," he said. "Shall I keep him in the—''

"No you won't keep me anywhere." A red-faced Jeremy, dressed in flashy tweeds, pushed his way past the butler and strode towards them. "Forget the tea party, Norton."

The butler's eyebrow rose as he glanced towards Charlie and with a helpless little gesture, she waved him away.

Jeremy's angry glance swung from Charlie's tear-stained face to Matt. "What the deuce is going on here? What have you been doing to upset Charlotte?"

"Matt hasn't upset me," she tried to explain.

"Of course he has," cried Jeremy, dragging her towards himself.

She shook her arm free of Jeremy's. "Don't make a fuss," she pleaded. But the two men stood glaring at each other—one thin, fair and red-faced, the other taller, broader, darkly angry. Both had their jaws thrust forward and their shoulders squared.

Jeremy snarled. "I'll make a fuss, all right. I'll have this fellow thrown off the estate!"

"How do you propose to do that?" Matt's eyes blazed and he clenched his fists against his thighs.

Oh, Lord! Charlie thought in alarm. Please don't let him lash out. He looks so angry!

Jeremy went even redder in the face and puffed out his thin chest like a ruffled rooster.

Matt continued his mocking challenge. "I suppose you have plenty of servants you can ask to toss me out. Why don't you go and rustle up a couple of gamekeepers or a footman with a cudgel?"

"Stop this!" cried Charlie, stepping between the two men. She held out her arms, warding them both off. "This is unnecessary."

"It certainly is," Matt spat out, stepping away from her. "I wasn't planning on hanging around any longer than I needed to and I've said what I came to say." His bleak gaze held hers for an agonising moment before he shook his head sadly, then turned his back to them both and strode defiantly out of the room.

"Matt! Don't go!" Charlie cried, unable to bear seeing him disappear. She stumbled across the room, but Jeremy grabbed her arm and pulled her back.

"He's nothing but an ill-bred thug. Let him go, sweetheart."

Wildly, she shouted. "You don't know the first thing about him." Struggling to push him away, she called again, "Matt!"

"It's obvious he's a red-necked cowboy who only knows how to argue with his fists."

"How dare you!" She managed to free her hands from his grasp at last and raced out of the room and down the hall with Jeremy hot on her heels.

They arrived at the front door just as Matt's motorbike took off with an angry roar. "Good riddance," muttered Jeremy.

"Shut up!" wailed Charlie. She was so angry and frustrated and filled with despair, she was sure her blood was boiling. "In fact, Jeremy!" she shouted as she watched his cheeks puff even more while his skin deepened to an impossible shade of red. "Why don't you—why don't you go do something you're really good at? Kick a corgi, or demolish a worker's cottage!"

Jeremy gaped then shut his mouth firmly.

A polite cough sounded in the doorway. "Lady Charlotte, would you like me to escort Lord Groves to his vehicle?"

"Oh, Norton, thank you." Charlie whispered, feeling dreadfully ill. "He's just leaving."

With a cold heart, she watched Jeremy's face and shoulders stiffen, before he followed Norton out of the house.

Like an automaton, Charlie wandered back into the east room, trying to come to terms with what had been said in the past hour.

Matt loved Charlie Bell.

A tiny corner of her breaking heart wanted to laugh and skip at that thought. If only she could *be* Charlie Bell. *Free to do as she liked.*

She sank into the nearest armchair and listlessly, her fingers traced its carved wooden arm. *She loved Matt Lockhart.* She knew that for certain. And she would probably never stop loving him. How terrible to think that for the rest of her life, she would never be able to think of Matt without also thinking, *what if?*

What if she wasn't a titled English lady?

What if her ancestors hadn't lumbered her family with this huge white elephant of a house?

What if she was free to choose her own mate?

"Lady Charlotte?"

She looked up to see Norton standing before her again, with a painting under his arm.

"What on earth are you up to now, Norton? Spring cleaning?"

"I thought you might like to see the gift Mr. Lockhart left for you."

CHAPTER SIX

"MATT brought me a painting?"

Charlie levered herself to sit upright in the chair as Norton carefully set the framed canvas on the mantelpiece in front of her.

It was the painting she loved most—the waterhole. *Their* waterhole.

Fresh tears filled her eyes, making the vibrant colours of the Outback blur as if the paint had run. Staring at Matt's painting, she could sense the sun-trapped heat of the rock beneath her and she could feel his arms around her once again. His mouth on hers, warm and seeking.

She swiped at her eyes. "Oh, Norton, isn't he the most amazing artist?"

"Quite remarkable," he agreed. Then after he'd stood beside her for a while, gazing at the painting in silent sympathy, he tiptoed out of the room leaving Charlie to her memories.

How painful they were. Heaven help her! When she had sat with Matt at that waterhole, she'd never felt so complete. It was as if she'd been waiting all her life to be in such a place, with such a man. With his hand in hers, she'd absorbed the atmosphere of peace and timelessness embraced by the ancient rocks.

As she thought about the tunnel through the rocks, the cave and the waterhole so far away, it occurred to her now, that they had existed long before Greenfields had been erected. And long after her family's stately home eventually crumbled and fell into ruins, Matt's special place on Sundown would still be there—a sanctuary for the animals and birds and for any lucky Lockhart descendants.

The difference between their worlds couldn't be greater, and yet she and Matt each had an inheritance and a responsibility...

She wept for her torn heart.

If only there were rules for falling in love! Then she could have avoided this terrible dilemma. But she had blithely walked into and out of a man's life in a matter of weeks. And that was all it had taken. Now she and Matt were left with a heartbreaking love that neither of them could do anything about.

After an age...she was all cried out.

Robot-like, she wandered upstairs to the bathroom, washed her face, brushed her hair and applied a little makeup to cover the puffiness under her eyes. And when she came downstairs again, she discovered her parents were home. Her mother had retired to rest and her father was in the east room making a huge fuss about the painting.

"Charlotte, sweetheart. Come and tell me all about this wonderful find."

"Daddy, how was Ambleside?"

"Lovely, darling," he replied vaguely. He gave his daughter the briefest of kisses before returning his attention to Matt's painting. He beckoned her closer. "Norton tells me some young Australian fellow painted this and gave it to you."

"Yes," she admitted and wished her heart wouldn't pump so frantically at the mere mention of Matt. "What do you think of it?"

"It's brilliant!" her father enthused. "This artist's use of colour is sensational, and he seems to have captured a kind of spiritual essence of the place somehow."

"He certainly has," she agreed softly.

"I find it riveting." Her father eyed her curiously. "Where did you find this fellow? In Sydney?"

"No," she said as she willed herself to stay calm and cool. "He actually lives way up near the border of Queensland

and the Northern Territory on a cattle property called Sundown.''

"Good heavens. So this place is on his land?''

"Yes.''

"Charlotte, what a find! You clever girl. What's his name? Has he done anything else?''

"He's called—Matt—Matthew Lockhart.'' Somehow she got the name out without faltering or sounding too tense. "And, yes there are plenty more paintings—some of them are huge and they're all very, very good.''

"And he wants to sell them over here and in Europe?''

"Oh, I don't know. We didn't discuss that.''

"You didn't? What's the matter with you, girl? Are you losing your touch? This is significant, new work. We need to snap this fellow up before someone else snaffles him. I can make him a fortune.''

"I'm not sure that he wants a fortune.''

"Of course he does. Everyone wants money. He needs a good agent.''

"You, of course,'' Charlie said with a faint smile. She knew her father was thinking of the wonderful commission he would make selling Matt's paintings—perhaps in time it would be almost enough to keep Greenfields out of the hands of the receivers.

"This talent needs nurturing, encouraging… Tell me more about this wonderful chap you've unearthed. How old is he? I hope he's youngish, plenty of time to mature and develop.''

She was beginning to feel rather frayed around the edges. Talking about Matt as if he was simply an artist and not the most important person in her life was too difficult. Drawing in a deep, shuddering breath, she tried to reply nonchalantly, "He—he's somewhere in his thirties. I didn't ask exactly.''

Her father switched his attention from the painting to his daughter. "Charlotte, what is it, dear? What's the matter?''

She blinked as her eyes threatened to overflow. "I'm feeling a little—oh, Daddy, I'm so miserable. I've fallen in love."

"Oh, dear," replied the earl nervously. "Come and sit down. You don't look too steady on your pins." He led his daughter to the big, soft sofa and they both sank into it. "Would you like me to fetch your mother?"

"Later," she whispered. "When I'm feeling stronger."

With long lean fingers, her father stroked the hair away from her cheek, slowly, gently. "Now tell me why falling in love should make my little girl so miserable."

"Because I fell in love with the wrong man," she sighed.

Her father's voice faltered just a little. "What's so wrong about him? Isn't he a decent sort of chap?"

"Oh, he's excessively decent."

"Has a good job? He could support you?"

"Yes. That's not the problem."

"He loves you?"

"Yes," she wailed and pressed her hands to her eyes, determined not to cry any more. "At least he loved Charlie Bell, but I'm not sure that he's too impressed with Charlotte Bellamy."

"I beg your pardon?" Her father was understandably puzzled. "My dear girl, what on earth do you mean?"

With a leaden heart, she explained the sorry story of her time on Sundown. To his credit, her father listened without interruption.

"I've known ever since I was little that I'm going to have to marry someone like Jeremy with scads of money and a title. It's the only way we're going to save Greenfields," she added.

Now it was her father's turn to let his jaw drop. She saw pain in his eyes. "You poor girl." Hugging her shoulders, he rocked her for several minutes. "Sweetheart, all your mother and I have ever wanted is for you to be happy. Perhaps we've given you the wrong impression. I suppose we assumed that your happiness would involve enjoying a certain lifestyle here in England. But, if I'm honest, I always suspected you'd make your own way…follow your own dream.''

''I've wrecked any chance of that,'' she said dully. ''I've lied and cheated…''

''We've let you down, darling. You shouldn't have had to go to such lengths to hide what you wanted to do so badly.''

''And now I've let Matt down. I can't bear it. He came all the way here to find me again and I—and I…''

Her father gave her shoulders a reassuring squeeze. ''I take it that this Matt of yours must also be Lockhart, the artist?'' His gaze shot back to the painting he so much admired.

Charlie smiled sadly. ''The very same.''

Her father's eyes glowed with poorly suppressed delight. He drew her head against his shoulder and ruffled her hair and sighed. ''He's probably not the type who forgives and forgets easily. I'm afraid you could be in for more disappointment when you go back. ''

''Go back?'' Charlie sighed. It was so tempting to think about leaping on a plane and dashing back to Australia. If she thought there was the slightest chance Matt would be pleased to see her, she wouldn't hesitate.

But a man like Matt had his pride.

''Of course, my dear. You're going to find young Lockhart and try to sort this mess out, aren't you?''

''I don't know if I'm brave enough. And I doubt it would be worth it,'' she whispered, her mind full of the memory of Matt's angry eyes and his stiff, stubborn back as he strode away from her.

''Of course you're brave,'' her father said, dropping a kiss on her forehead. ''And I know you. You will go.''

Stripped to the waist, Matt was painting up a storm. His brush flashed in fierce, passionate strokes across the canvas.

He'd never painted this way before, pouring all his feelings out in a frenzied burst of colour and emotion. Usually painting soothed and restored him.

Today, the more he painted the worse he felt, but he couldn't stop. He was possessed by a sense of desperation that wouldn't let him go. On a semiconscious level, his brain was selecting colours and making choices about line and balance and shape, but for the most part his mind was completely filled with Charlie.

He hadn't been able to free himself from the shock of discovering she was really Lady Charlotte Bellamy. If he'd arrived in England and been told by Norton that she'd run away to live with seven dwarfs, it wouldn't have been as bad as seeing her sailing off to the opera on the arm of that wimp, Lord Groves. And wearing that magnificent green dress.

Now he was trying to capture the transformation from Charlie Bell to English Lady. Combined on the canvas were images of *his* Charlie with her jodhpurs and riding boots and her soft, brown plait hanging over one shoulder and Lady Charlotte with her golden hair, velvet gown and creamy white, touch-me-feel-me skin. Maybe by the time he was finished, he would be able to get them both out of his system.

He worked in a studio he'd added to the back of Sundown homestead some years ago. Built lean-to style, with a skylight in the roof, the area had floor to ceiling louvers on the three external walls. Scattered around the room were easels, rolls of canvas, tins of paint and mineral turpentine and various-sized frames stacked against one wall.

For ease of movement, he'd shed his shirt and tossed it over a three-legged stool. He preferred to stand, so that he could use his whole body to add movement to the brush as he worked. When he painted really hard like he was today, he poured an enormous amount of physical energy into the canvas.

The barking of a dog penetrated his concentration and he looked up, frowning. His ears were attuned to the usual sounds of an Outback station—the constant hum of the electric generator, the clanging of gate chains from the yards nearby, the putter and spurt of the latest motor the mechanic was working on. But above all that, he could also hear the approach of a vehicle, still some distance away.

The mail truck, no doubt. At least he didn't need to stop work. Arch was spending the morning going over the books in the office and he would collect the mail and have a cup of tea and a yarn with the mailman. Matt had left strict instructions that he didn't want to be disturbed.

Daubing thick green paint, mixed so dark it was almost black, he filled in the shadows on Lady Charlotte's evening gown. Shadows made the womanliness of her figure come to warm life. As each tender curve emerged, a painful memory resurfaced, but he had to push on. When he finished this painting, he could be finished with Charlie Bell.

He heard Arch's heavy step as he went out onto the veranda to meet the mailman. Poor Arch had been pretty cut up when Matt returned from England alone. The head stockman had been so hopeful that if his boss simply turned up in Derbyshire, in two shakes he'd be coming home to Sundown with Charlie as his bride. What a joke!

The laugh of the millennium!

Instead, when Matt had come home, he and Arch had spent several days and nights listing the many blessings of a bachelor's life, while drowning their sorrows and their bafflement in rum.

Selecting a smaller brush, Matt began to fill in the green of Charlie's eyes. As with the dress, he added darker tones to give them depth. He worked intently for some minutes, but suddenly his hand stilled. A ghostly chill crept along his spine. She was looking back at him.

Out of the canvas, Charlie's eyes held his. Wistful, worried eyes. Eyes that still wanted him. Eyes that tore at his heart, his gut, his groin. Groaning, he threw down the brush.

And looked up.

The eyes were still there. Haunting him.

Watching him from the far side of the room.

He blinked and his pulse raced. He couldn't tell what the hell had happened to his legs. Their bones seemed to have vaporised. "Charlie?"

"Hello, Matt." She stood in the doorway, her eyes as worried and wistful as the ones he'd just painted. Her face was very pale.

"What are—? How did you get here?"

Her beautiful soft lips twitched into a nervous smile. "The same way I always get to this place—on the mail truck."

Wildly he rammed paint-stained fingers through his hair, as his heart pounded. "That was a darn foolish thing to do." Stooping to snatch up a rag, he began to scrub at the stains on his hands. He spoke without looking at her. "You'd better go out to the kitchen. I'm sure Arch will give you a cup of tea and then you can hop straight back on that truck and clear off again."

"I'm not getting back on any truck till I've finished my business," she said quietly.

Her determined voice softened by that pretty English lilt, impelled him to look at her. "What business would that be?"

"I had to come to thank you for the painting."

"A polite little thank-you note would have been fine." His attempt at a laugh turned into a snort.

She dropped her gaze and he watched, fascinated, as her thick, dark lashes rested against her cheeks. Those rosy cheeks of hers were a lethal weapon and Matt could feel his throat damming up.

"I've come all this way from England to talk to you."

"Yeah. I know all about that trip. I've done it myself and it was a waste of time and effort for me, too."

"Matt, I've come to ask you to forgive me."

He had to admit the woman had guts. While he shook in his boots, she stood in front of him, looking cool as a cucumber with her fresh white blouse tucked neatly into her jeans and her hair hanging over her shoulder in a single plait. Only now her braided hair was the colour of golden wheat.

This new combination of Charlie Bell and Lady Charlotte was quite something to look at! He stood clutching the paint rag, his eyes hungrily taking in details—the green of her eyes was the green of the deepest rock pool; her lips, so soft and full were designed to drive a man crazy.

He couldn't afford to look at her! His mind turned to mush when he did that. Spinning on his heel, he walked away to the far side of the room.

Charlie watched Matt's retreating back with a quaking heart. Seeing him again was so much worse than she expected. The jolt of longing that slammed into her when she first caught sight of his dark head bent low over his work had been frightening in its intensity.

And now there was this awful silence! She had expected he would be mad at her, but she thought he would argue. A heated debate she could handle. But the grim silence of this half-dressed man was alarming.

She ran her tongue over her lips. "I came to apologise properly," she told him, and took a tentative step forward. Before she lost her nerve, she added, "I'm here to stay if you'll have me. If you can forgive me."

His only answer was a stiffening of that beautiful, broad, brown back. With a sigh, she sent out a fervent prayer for help. How on earth could she regain Matt's trust? Wasn't he going to give her a chance to explain?

Her gaze fell on the easel he'd been using. "You're working on a new painting?"

That brought him whirling back to face her. He lunged forward as if he'd like to snatch it up before she could see it. "It's still very preliminary."

"Is it another Outback scene? My father was very taken with your painting of the waterhole. He thinks you have a magnificent talent. Wants to be your agent and make you a fortune."

"You don't say."

Stepping closer to the easel, she caught sight of the frenzied splashes of colour in his latest work. "Oh, my goodness, Matt." Its boldness left her breathless, as if she'd been winded. This painting was more abstract, more wild than his usual style, but quite, quite brilliant. But it was the subject matter that stole her breath and sent her heart hammering.

His rueful chuckle sounded beside her and he cocked an elbow at the painting. "This is a new kind of aversion therapy. I'm painting you out of my system."

"Is it working?" she whispered.

"Like a charm," he replied with a sad smile. He squinted at the canvas and then at a clock on the wall. "By my calculations, I should be completely over you by about five o'clock this afternoon."

His voice sounded hard and bitter, but when he looked at her, his dark eyes shimmered with telltale emotions.

She almost wept. "You want me out of your system, Matt?" Reaching out, she bravely touched his bare brown arm with her fingertips.

"You bet I do." He stared down at her fingers resting there. Their gentle pressure was like exquisite torture. But it was just as painful to witness her courage and her willingness to risk being hurt. Matt had been there and done that and it was a place he had no wish to visit a second time. "My sanity needs you out of my system," he told her with a scowl.

Reaching over, he snatched up his shirt from where it lay across the stool.

Charlie couldn't help herself.

Hungrily, she studied the play of muscles in his stomach and chest as he hauled the shirt over his head and she knew by the way Matt's eyes glinted that he was aware of her interest in his bare skin. Despite his anger, his gaze sparked sensuous heat as he did the buttons up slowly. One by one. Starting from the bottom, he closed the shirt at a leisurely pace until every tantalising inch of toned and suntanned flesh was covered by light blue cotton.

She hoped her tongue hadn't trailed lustily over her lips while she watched, but she couldn't be sure.

Straightening her shoulders, she dragged in a deep breath, lifted her chin and challenged him. "You at least owe me the chance to explain why I'm here. When you came to visit me, you got to say your piece, so you should hear me out."

Grim-mouthed, he dragged the stool across the floor and offered it to her. "Take a seat."

She accepted it and sat before her legs gave way. He fetched another stool from the far corner of the room. Then straddling it, he crossed his arms over his chest and eyed her steadily. "You said you've come to stay, but it can't work."

"How can you be so sure?"

"I can't change who I am and you can't change who you are. We've got responsibilities to our families and to the lives we've been born into, Lady Charlotte."

Sitting stiffly on the stool, her hands twisted in anxious knots. "What about a compromise? From what I can see, living in the Outback seems to be full of compromise."

"I can't imagine what you're driving at." His face darkened.

Charlie watched the crimson tide sweep up his neck. "When you came to England, you said you loved Charlie Bell," she whispered, her heart rocking wildly in her chest, like a fragile boat on a very stormy sea.

"I did."

"Then surely we can think up new ways of looking at this problem." She leaned forward and her voice shook as she asked, "Can't you also fall in love with Lady Charlotte?"

He sighed. "How can we overcome the huge differences in our lifestyles? I'm an Outback cattleman. I can't ever be someone like Jeremy."

She almost laughed out loud. "Oh, Matt! Thank heavens for that. I don't want anyone like Jeremy. I want you. I want here." Then, gaining no responding smile from him, Charlie drew in a shuddering breath and dredged up her bravest grin. "You're sounding so—so un-Australian. We British are supposed to be the ones who cling to outdated class systems. Not you."

Her teeth gnawed at her lower lip. This was it—time to face the music. "I have to know once and for all, Matt—don't you want me?"

He jumped to his feet. "That's not a fair question." Anger flared in his eyes and in his voice. "I can't have you." He strode to the door. "Honestly, Charlie, you're wasting your time. We shouldn't be dragging ourselves through the misery of this useless discussion. I'm going to get Arch and tell him to hold that mail truck for you."

Horrified, Charlie watched him disappear through the doorway. The man she loved was walking out of her life for the second time. *No way!*

"Matt!" she cried, running after him. "Wait! I have something important to say."

In the doorway, he reappeared and hovered, frowning at her. Without speaking, he rested one hand high on the lintel as if he'd only come back to hear her out and would push off again at any minute.

She had no idea where her courage came from, but she stepped towards him. "What if I—what if I were to offer you an indecent proposal?"

His eyes widened. "An *indecent* proposal?" In spite of his tension, the corners of his mouth twitched. His arms lowered to cross over his chest and he rested a bulky shoulder against the door frame. "OK. You have my undivided attention."

"It's simple really. You should have two women in your life."

Matt let out a disheartening chuckle. "I take it we're talking about Charlie Bell and Lady Charlotte Bellamy?"

"Yes." Her hands fluttered helplessly in front of her. "Couldn't you think of me as Charlie Bell when I'm here with you for the rest of our lives? And then couldn't you try to put up with Lady Charlotte when we visit my home in England?"

He stopped chuckling. His throat worked. "What was that you said about the *rest of our lives?* Can you run that by me again?"

"It's just a suggestion," she said with a self-conscious shrug of her shoulders. If only he would take her into his arms, she was certain any doubts would shrivel to nothing. "I thought that stubborn Matt Lockhart, the bush legend, would be sure to recognise a good deal when he sees it. I'm offering two women for the price of one."

His arms uncrossed and he stood straight, looking down at her. "I *am* giving it some thought."

"Don't worry about Lady Charlotte, if you don't want her. Charlie Bell is the real me. I never felt happier, more—*myself* than I did when I was working here. And I have my parents' blessing to come back to you."

He took a step towards her.

"What do you think, Matt?"

"I'm thinking… I'm actually thinking that perhaps I could handle having two women in my life."

"Of course you could."

This time his face broke into a slow grin. "I'm thinking about how I rather liked the look of that Lady Charlotte. She was one class act as I remember." He took two more steps. "I seem to recall that full, sexy mouth of hers. It looked great with lipstick. And I was rather taken with a very impressive neckline…and her eyes…'' He reached out and took her trembling hands. ''…suggesting an inner fire…''

Charlie knew all about the inner fire he described. At this very moment, her innards were close to meltdown.

He pulled her closer. ''I guess I could give your idea my best shot.''

Unable to hold back a second longer, she closed the gap and was finally in the circle of his arms. ''Oh, Matt.''

Whatever else she wanted to say was silenced as he took her mouth in a kiss that was everything she'd been waiting for…and more. With a groan of impatience, his mouth claimed hers and his hands clasped her possessively against him. It was a long, hungry embrace that left them both breathless and shaky.

''Talk about fire,'' Matt whispered.

''Stop lusting after Lady Charlotte,'' she murmured against his lips. ''I've already told you, Charlie is the real me.''

''Yeah.'' His lips grazed hers. ''I'm more than happy to settle for Charlie.''

He kissed her again, slowly, deeply, pouring his love into the act.

''Matt,'' she whispered when they stopped for breath. ''Am I forgiven?''

He pressed his forehead against hers and his big hands gripped her hips, holding her close. ''As soon as I looked up and saw you, I suspected I was gone. The minute you started talking about the rest of our lives, I forgot why I thought you should leave.''

''So you'll let me stay?''

''You have to stay!'' he growled against her throat. ''Promise you'll not run away again?''

''Cross my heart.'' With one hand she traced the sign of the cross across her breast.

Matt smiled. ''Can I do that?'' He drew slow, heated lines over both her breasts and then back the other way.

Charlie shivered deliciously.

"I love you, Charlie Bell. I love the look of you and the feel of you." His hands rose to her shoulders and his eyes looked deeply into hers. "But I think I love your determination even more. I have a feeling I'll be grateful for that for the rest of my life."

She rested her hand against his cheek. "I can't help being determined. I'm head over heels in love with you, Matt Lockhart."

"This indecent proposal of yours," he murmured. "Did you have any plans for making it decent? Like a—a wedding or something?"

Her eyebrow arched provocatively. "A girl can't do all the running. I know you're a man of few words, but I'll leave that move to you."

"I feel a bit pretentious proposing marriage to a lady."

Charlie sighed and punched him playfully on the shoulder. "Lady Charlotte is stuck in England, you silly man. Try asking Charlie Bell and see what happens."

His mouth quirked. "Charlie?"

"Yes?" Her answer was the merest hush of sound.

"Do you fancy being the missus of an Outback cattleman?"

"Oh, yes," she replied more definitely.

He laughed happily. "Thank you." Scooping her into his arms, he showered her with loving kisses.

She smiled. "Thank *you* for the best decent proposal I've ever had."

"So it's a bush wedding, then?"

"Yes, why not?"

Matt chuckled. "I'd like to see Norton at a barbecue drinking billy tea."

"Well, the alternative is Arch in a top hat and tails in the Greenfields chapel."

"Either way, it doesn't matter, as long as you're there."

Happier than she ever thought possible, Charlie wound her arms around his neck and kissed him back.

THE AUSTRALIANS

MEN WHO TURN YOUR WHOLE WORLD UPSIDE DOWN!

Look out for novels about the Wonder from Down Under—where spirited women win the hearts of Australia's most eligible men.

Harlequin Romance®:

OUTBACK WITH THE BOSS
Barbara Hannay (September, #3670)

MASTER OF MARAMBA
Margaret Way (October, #3671)

OUTBACK FIRE
Margaret Way (December, #3678)

Harlequin Presents®:

A QUESTION OF MARRIAGE
Lindsay Armstrong (October, #2208)

FUGITIVE BRIDE
Miranda Lee (November, #2212)

Available wherever Harlequin books are sold.

HARLEQUIN®
Makes any time special ®

Harlequin truly does make any time special. . . . This year we are celebrating weddings in style!

To help us celebrate, we want you to tell us how wearing the Harlequin wedding gown will make your wedding day special. As the grand prize, Harlequin will offer one lucky bride the chance to **"Walk Down the Aisle"** in the Harlequin wedding gown!

There's more...

For her honeymoon, she and her groom will spend five nights at the **Hyatt Regency Maui.** As part of this five-night honeymoon at the hotel renowned for its romantic attractions, the couple will enjoy a candlelit dinner for two in Swan Court, a sunset sail on the hotel's catamaran, and duet spa treatments.

A HYATT RESORT AND SPA® Maui • Molokai • Lanai

To enter, please write, in, 250 words or less, how wearing the Harlequin wedding gown will make your wedding day special. The entry will be judged based on its emotionally compelling nature, its originality and creativity, and its sincerity. This contest is open to Canadian and U.S. residents only and to those who are 18 years of age and older. There is no purchase necessary to enter. Void where prohibited. See further contest rules attached. Please send your entry to:

Walk Down the Aisle Contest

In Canada	In U.S.A.
P.O. Box 637	P.O. Box 9076
Fort Erie, Ontario	3010 Walden Ave.
L2A 5X3	Buffalo, NY 14269-9076

You can also enter by visiting www.eHarlequin.com
Win the Harlequin wedding gown and the vacation of a lifetime!
The deadline for entries is October 1, 2001.

HARLEQUIN®
Makes any time special ®

HARLEQUIN WALK DOWN THE AISLE TO MAUI CONTEST 1197
OFFICIAL RULES
NO PURCHASE NECESSARY TO ENTER

1. To enter, follow directions published in the offer to which you are responding. Contest begins April 2, 2001, and ends on October 1, 2001. Method of entry may vary. Mailed entries must be postmarked by October 1, 2001, and received by October 8, 2001.

2. Contest entry may be, at times, presented via the Internet, but will be restricted solely to residents of certain geographic areas that are disclosed on the Web site. To enter via the Internet, if permissible, access the Harlequin Web site (www.eHarlequin.com) and follow the directions displayed online. Online entries must be received by 11:59 p.m. E.S.T. on October 1, 2001.

   In lieu of submitting an entry online, enter by mail by hand-printing (or typing) on an 8½" x 11" plain piece of paper, your name, address (including zip code), Contest number/name and in 250 words or fewer, why winning a Harlequin wedding dress would make your wedding day special. Mail via first-class mail to: Harlequin Walk Down the Aisle Contest 1197, (in the U.S.) P.O. Box 9076, 3010 Walden Avenue, Buffalo, NY 14269-9076, (in Canada) P.O. Box 637, Fort Erie, Ontario L2A 5X3, Canada.

   Limit one entry per person, household address and e-mail address. Online and/or mailed entries received from persons residing in geographic areas in which Internet entry is not permissible will be disqualified.

3. Contests will be judged by a panel of members of the Harlequin editorial, marketing and public relations staff based on the following criteria:

   - Originality and Creativity—50%
   - Emotionally Compelling—25%
   - Sincerity—25%

   In the event of a tie, duplicate prizes will be awarded. Decisions of the judges are final.

4. All entries become the property of Torstar Corp. and will not be returned. No responsibility is assumed for lost, late, illegible, incomplete, inaccurate, nondelivered or misdirected mail or misdirected e-mail, for technical, hardware or software failures of any kind, lost or unavailable network connections, or failed, incomplete, garbled or delayed computer transmission or any human error which may occur in the receipt or processing of the entries in this Contest.

5. Contest open only to residents of the U.S. (except Puerto Rico) and Canada, who are 18 years of age or older, and is void wherever prohibited by law; all applicable laws and regulations apply. Any litigation within the Province of Quebec respecting the conduct or organization of a publicity contest may be submitted to the Régie des alcools, des courses et des jeux for a ruling. Any litigation respecting the awarding of a prize may be submitted to the Régie des alcools, des courses et des jeux only for the purpose of helping the parties reach a settlement. Employees and immediate family members of Torstar Corp. and D. L. Blair, Inc., their affiliates, subsidiaries and all other agencies, entities and persons connected with the use, marketing or conduct of this Contest are not eligible to enter. Taxes on prizes are the sole responsibility of winners. Acceptance of any prize offered constitutes permission to use winner's name, photograph or other likeness for the purposes of advertising, trade and promotion on behalf of Torstar Corp., its affiliates and subsidiaries without further compensation to the winner, unless prohibited by law.

6. Winners will be determined no later than November 15, 2001, and will be notified by mail. Winners will be required to sign and return an Affidavit of Eligibility form within 15 days after winner notification. Noncompliance within that time period may result in disqualification and an alternative winner may be selected. Winners of trip must execute a Release of Liability prior to ticketing and must possess required travel documents (e.g. passport, photo ID) where applicable. Trip must be completed by November 2002. No substitution of prize permitted by winner. Torstar Corp. and D. L. Blair, Inc., their parents, affiliates, and subsidiaries are not responsible for errors in printing or electronic presentation of Contest, entries and/or game pieces. In the event of printing or other errors which may result in unintended prize values or duplication of prizes, all affected game pieces or entries shall be null and void. If for any reason the Internet portion of the Contest is not capable of running as planned, including infection by computer virus, bugs, tampering, unauthorized intervention, fraud, technical failures, or any other causes beyond the control of Torstar Corp. which corrupt or affect the administration, secrecy, fairness, integrity or proper conduct of the Contest, Torstar Corp. reserves the right, at its sole discretion, to disqualify any individual who tampers with the entry process and to cancel, terminate, modify or suspend the Contest or the Internet portion thereof. In the event of a dispute regarding an online entry, the entry will be deemed submitted by the authorized holder of the e-mail account submitted at the time of entry. Authorized account holder is defined as the natural person who is assigned to an e-mail address by an Internet access provider, online service provider or other organization that is responsible for arranging e-mail address for the domain associated with the submitted e-mail address. **Purchase or acceptance of a product offer does not improve your chances of winning.**

7. Prizes: (1) Grand Prize—A Harlequin wedding dress (approximate retail value: $3,500) and a 5-night/6-day honeymoon trip to Maui, HI, including round-trip air transportation provided by Maui Visitors Bureau from Los Angeles International Airport (winner is responsible for transportation to and from Los Angeles International Airport) and a Harlequin Romance Package, including hotel accomodations (double occupancy) at the Hyatt Regency Maui Resort and Spa, dinner for (2) two at Swan Court, a sunset sail on Kiele V and a spa treatment for the winner (approximate retail value: $4,000); (5) Five runner-up prizes of a $1000 gift certificate to selected retail outlets to be determined by Sponsor (retail value $1000 ea.). Prizes consist of only those items listed as part of the prize. Limit one prize per person. All prizes are valued in U.S. currency.

8. For a list of winners (available after December 17, 2001) send a self-addressed, stamped envelope to: Harlequin Walk Down the Aisle Contest 1197 Winners, P.O. Box 4200 Blair, NE 68009-4200 or you may access the www.eHarlequin.com Web site through January 15, 2002.

Contest sponsored by Torstar Corp., P.O. Box 9042, Buffalo, NY 14269-9042, U.S.A.

PHWDACONT2

TO HAVE AND TO HOLD

Marriages meant to last!

They've already said "I do," but what happens
when their promise to love, honor and cherish
is put to the test?

Emotions run high as husbands and wives
discover how precious—and fragile—
their wedding vows are....
Will true love keep them together—forever?

Look out in Harlequin Romance® for:

HUSBAND FOR A YEAR
Rebecca Winters (August, #3665)

THE MARRIAGE TEST
Barbara McMahon (September, #3669)

HIS TROPHY WIFE
Leigh Michaels (October, #3672)

THE WEDDING DEAL
Janelle Denison (November, #3678)

PART-TIME MARRIAGE
Jessica Steele (December, #3680)

Available wherever Harlequin books are sold.

HARLEQUIN®
Makes any time special ®

Visit us at www.eHarlequin.com   HRTHATHR